THE TERRIBLE SECRETS OF THE TELL-ALL CLUB

BY CATHERINE STIER

Albert Whitman & Company
Morton Grove, Illinois

Library of Congress Cataloging-in-Publication Data

Stier, Catherine.
The terrible secrets of the Tell-All Club / by Catherine Stier.
p. cm.
Summary: When four fifth-grade friends complete a "tell-all" survey,
tensions arise and come to a head during an overnight class trip.
ISBN 978-0-8075-7798-1
[1. Interpersonal relations—Fiction. 2. Friendship—Fiction. 3. Self-
confidence—Fiction. 4. Clubs—Fiction. 5. Schools—Fiction.] I. Title.
PZ7.S8556295Te 2009
[Fic]—dc22
2008055704

Cover by Shane Clester and Nick Tiemersma.

The design is by Nick Tiemersma.

For more information about Albert Whitman & Company,
visit our web site at www.albertwhitman.com.

To the Script Sisters.

TABLE OF CONTENTS

PART 2 — All Together Now: Camp Kindred Spirits

PROLOGUE

Kiley pushed back a blond wisp and stared at the question she had just typed on the computer. *One down*, she thought. *But so many more to go*. And the possibilities were endless.

Kiley smiled to herself. She knew her new club would be the best club, the one everyone—girls *and* guys—would want to join. After all wasn't she, Kiley, the club's creator, one of the most popular kids in school?

And another thing. This wouldn't be like all those other clubs kids were always putting together. This one was way more original. No one at Harper Lee Elementary had ever, *ever* thought up a club like this.

Now came the tricky part. Coming up with the questions for the kids who wanted to join. Kiley knew what she REALLY wanted to ask. But not yet. That would come last. That would be Question 50.

The first question, the one she'd just typed, was fluff, just to get everyone started.

Question 1: What is your favorite salad dressing?

What else can I ask? Kiley mused. Something simple, something that wouldn't scare anyone off. She poked at the keys again.

Question 2: What is your favorite T.V. show?

It's getting easier, Kiley thought. She typed more quickly.

Question 3: What is your favorite color?

Question 4: What are your favorite pizza toppings?

Question 5: What sports do you totally love to play?

Then Kiley decided to get more creative. More nosy, too.

Question 6: Out of all the stores at the mall, where do you like to shop?

Question 7: What is your favorite memory?

Question 8: What music you like best—
rock or rap or pop?

Question 9: If you hung up a poster in your room or
locker, who or what would be on the poster?

Question 10: How many parties did you go to last year?

At the rate she was going, Kiley knew she'd be typing in Question 50, the one she really cared about, very soon.

And Kiley knew something else. Anyone who wanted to be in the club would have to answer ALL the questions. Even the last one, the BIG one, Question 50. That was the most important rule of the new club.

And the whole reason it was called the Tell-All Club.

CHAPTER 1

Josh Bendle, Bogus Super Fan

Tell-All Question 5: What sports do you totally love to play?

Josh stood in his driveway, shivering.

This one, I'll make.

He eyed the basket mounted over the garage door. If he could sink it, finally sink it, he would have earned what he craved: rest, warmth, relief.

Josh tried to steady his shaking body. The basketball arced, hit the edge of the rim and ricocheted away. Josh had to chase it down his icy driveway.

Josh had never been a basketball fan, not even a sports fan, really. But ever since they installed outdoor basketball nets at school last summer, that was all the fifth-grade boys did at lunchtime. Even now, in February, with boots and heavy jackets weighing them down, the boys played endless games of basketball. And Josh was tired of being the worst on the court.

Well, not the worst, maybe, he thought. But pretty bad. Not like that kid in his class, T.J. Mariani. T.J. had such incredible natural talent that he could toss the ball and sink it while hardly glancing at the net at all.

This time, Josh tried flinging the ball from the end of his driveway, practicing his three-pointers. The ball missed by a mile, clanging against a gutter. Not even close. Josh sighed. He was on basket number nine. Just one more to go, one more, and he could walk through the front door, nuke himself a cup of hot chocolate, and wrap his fingers around the steaming cup until they thawed.

And what had brought on all this self-torture? A promise he had made to himself.

Months ago, Josh had vowed he'd shoot till he made ten baskets, every day after school. No matter the weather. And on weekends, too. He had pretty much stuck to the bargain he'd struck with himself.

Funny thing, though. Ever since he started, Josh had heard that the whole neighborhood thought he was a basketball nut, some kind of super fan. His family seemed to think so, too. For his birthday two weeks ago, his relatives had given him basketball team jerseys, a basketball player bobble head, and all kinds of other basketball gear.

Really, Josh hated basketball.

He hated the feeling that he was being forced to

become an expert at something he couldn't care less about. Just to fit in. There were only about a thousand things he'd rather be doing right now. Even homework was better—way better—than shooting baskets.

But who wanted to be tormented every day at lunch recess for being completely hopeless on the court, all year long?

Not me.

Josh aimed again at the net.

He shot, missed again.

Grumbling under his breath, he turned to chase the ball—and bumped into Anne Park.

At least, he thought it was Anne. Whoever it was, she was so bundled up he could see only two big brown eyes above a big pink scarf.

"Uhhh...sorry," Josh said. The girl pulled down her scarf and smiled. It was Anne, after all. She was a friend, a fifth-grader like he was, but in a different classroom.

"That's okay," said Anne. "You're sure practicing a lot."

Josh felt his cheeks grow hot. How many missed shots had Anne seen as she came down the walk? "Yeah," Josh mumbled, then to change the subject, "You going to Kiley's?"

He tipped his head toward the house next door.

Anne nodded. "We're going to work on homework together. And valentines."

"Oh," said Josh. "Okay."

He didn't know what else to say. But Anne still stood there.

She was still standing there when Josh heard the automatic garage door motor begin to rumble. Anne suddenly spoke in a rush over the noise. "Did Kiley tell you about the club she's starting..."

Josh barely heard her words because he was turning, turning toward the rumbling, turning toward the opening garage door. Then he cringed. Steve-O stood there. Big, sloppy, sneering Steve-O. Steve-O was the worst sixth-grader in all of Harper Lee Elementary—and, as luck would have it, Josh's big brother.

Josh knew what was coming.

"Am I interrupting something?" asked Steve-O, in a mocking baby-voice. "Were you and Annie-poo having a little lovey-dovey chat?"

Josh could feel his face grow even hotter.

"Gotta go," blurted Anne, and she turned quickly toward Kiley's house.

"Geez. Can you be more obvious? You soooo like her," Steve-O accused, none too quietly.

"Nah," Josh growled.

"Yeah, you do. You should see your face! It's all red," Steve-O said.

"I told you, I don't like her," Josh snapped back.

"I think you're in love with Annie-poo!"

Shut up, thought Josh, *Shut up, shut up, shut up*. But he shouted, "Clam it, Steve-O. I can hardly stand her!"

As soon as the words sputtered out of his mouth, Josh regretted them. He had only wanted to quiet Steve-O. He didn't mean a word of it. Anne was nice—he liked Anne, really he did. He turned and saw Anne hurrying up Kiley's front steps, and felt a sickening little twist in his stomach.

Did Anne hear Steve-O? he wondered.

Did she hear me?

Could she hear anything through that big pink scarf?

CHAPTER 2

Anne Park, Perfect Poser

Tell-All Question 18: Who is your BFF?

Anne flew into Kiley's house as soon as Kiley opened the door. Anne knew her face must have turned pale, as it always did when she was upset. She hoped Kiley wouldn't notice. She did, of course.

"What's up with you? You look sick," Kiley said, shoving the door closed against the cold.

"Nothing," Anne answered quickly. "Hey, I've been thinking. You know that idea you had, to start a club again? And this time to invite boys to join? Maybe… maybe that's not such a great idea."

Kiley shrugged. "Just thought it would make things more interesting to have T.J. and some other guys around. And you're the one who suggested we ask Josh, that basketball nut neighbor of mine," she reminded her.

"But whatever. Did you bring your books, Anne? And your valentines? We can sign them after homework."

"Yeah." Anne kicked off her boots in the foyer, unwrapped her pink scarf, and pulled off her hat. Her black shiny hair tumbled down her back.

Kiley shook her head at her. "You know, whenever I pull off a hat, all my hair sticks straight up in a static nightmare," said Kiley, touching her own shorter blond cut. "How did you get such perfect hair?"

Anne reached a hand back to her hair, almost embarrassed. "Oh, it's not perfect."

"Definitely perfect," Kiley said. "Well, c'mon. Let's go tackle that homework. Mr. Garcia really dumped it on us today."

"Yeah, my teacher did, too," said Anne.

Anne shrugged off her coat and followed Kiley as her mind tried to shrug off something else.

It wouldn't have hurt so much if it had been anyone else who yelled that awful thing, Anne thought. She still heard, echoing in her head, those terrible words: *Clam it, Steve-O. I can hardly stand her!* But not Josh. Not Josh Bendle.

As Kiley spread her books on the kitchen table, Anne struggled to keep from crying.

Anne remembered how when she had moved to this town in third grade, hardly anyone had been nice to her. Not that anyone had been mean, either. They just hadn't noticed her.

But Josh saw her on the very first day in the hallway at Harper Lee Elementary. Anne was so nervous about being new that she had gotten sick to her stomach. Her teacher had sent her to the nurse's office. Only, when she left the classroom, Anne didn't know where the nurse's office was. Too embarrassed to return to class, she stood there, looking blankly around the hall like a lost kindergartner. Then this dark-haired, green-eyed boy had come walking toward her.

"You okay?" he asked softly.

"No," she said. "I need to see the nurse."

"Whoa," he said simply. "Follow me." And she had. He led her to the little nurse's room tucked, as Anne figured she should have guessed, inside the main office.

And after that, they talked at recess and she found out his name was Josh, Josh Bendle, and he seemed so kind. She learned they were in the same grade, just different classes. They lived pretty close, too. And, after that first day, they sometimes walked to school together.

Then something really weird happened. Anne's mother talked Anne into letting her hair grow long the summer before fifth grade. So Anne had. But who knew it would grow so fast, and come in all shiny, and fall down her back like some kind of silky curtain? Suddenly, people began noticing Anne. People who had never really bothered with her before. Popular kids. People like Kiley.

Secretly, Anne wasn't completely comfortable with

this new popularity. Sometimes Anne felt like she was just pretending to be one of Kiley's crowd. And a tiny part of her couldn't help wondering if all it would take to make her new friends disappear was one bad haircut.

Josh, though, had been different. He had been a real friend, before the others had suddenly started paying attention to her. He had always been someone she could count on. Or so she had thought till five minutes ago.

Suddenly Kiley slammed her book shut, and Anne jumped.

"I see you're not interested in division now," said Kiley. "And I agree. Sooo..." Kiley's eyebrows lifted. "Let's talk about our club," she said.

"Uhhh..."

"I think we need to make this club something different, something special."

"Different?" Anne asked cautiously. "What kind of different?"

Kiley's mom walked in the room then, the cordless phone tucked between her chin and shoulder. She turned to load a few glasses into the dishwasher.

Kiley's mom nodded her head as she spoke into the receiver. "Yeah, the book's okay. Not exactly material for our book club," she said. "More like a Hollywood tell-all. Lots of secrets spilled."

Anne watched Kiley's eyes grow wide at her mom's words.

"That's it," Kiley whispered. "A Tell-All Club!"

CHAPTER 3

Kiley Dryden, Sly Spy

Tell-All Question 23: What is your least favorite holiday?

Two days later, Kiley watched a pink gift bow fall to the floor. "Oh, Hunter," her sister Ginger squealed. "You are too sweet!" Then Kiley heard kissy-kissy sounds.

From where she crouched under the dining room table, Kiley could only see her sister's legs and Hunter's jeans hanging out from under the tablecloth—and their shoes, of course. Although they sat in different chairs, Hunter's sneakered foot was mashed right next to one of Ginger's ballet flats.

It was Valentine's Day. The first Valentine's Day that Ginger, now sixteen, had a "real" boyfriend. When Hunter came to their house with two presents sloppily wrapped in white tissue printed with red hearts, Kiley had been chased out of the dining room. But Kiley had crawled back in on her hands and knees and hidden under the dining room table. This was just too good to be missed.

Now she heard a rustling, the sound of tissue paper being moved aside. "Oh, Hunter. It's sooo cute," Ginger cooed. Kiley watched Ginger plop something onto her lap. She could just make it out—an adorable stuffed animal, a dark brown teddy bear wearing a red ribbon with gold letters. "To My Honey," the letters spelled out. Kiley silently sighed. Would anyone ever give *her* such a wonderful Valentine's Day present?

Suddenly, Ginger shifted her weight. As she moved, her foot came crashing into Kiley as she crouched in her hiding place.

"Who's there?" Ginger hollered. The tablecloth flew up, and Kiley found herself eye to eye with her furious sister.

"Get out of here you, little fungus," her sister said in a deadly voice. And Kiley took off, scurrying out from under the table. But as she careened out of the dining room, Kiley took one last backward glance and saw that her sister was also clutching a big, red gorgeous heart-shaped box of chocolates topped with a gigantic bow.

Kiley headed inside her bedroom, slamming the door behind her. She flopped on the floor and stared glumly at the ceiling. Then she reached into the bag of valentines she'd received that afternoon at the class Valentine's Day party. Slowly she unfolded the valentines from her classmates. The first one was from her next-door neighbor. He had signed the sports-designed valentine simply "Josh" and had taped on a wrapped piece of bubble gum. *Good old Josh*, Kiley thought as she unfastened, then unwrapped the gum and popped it in her mouth.

Kiley reached for another valentine, then another. *This is stupid*, she thought as she pulled each tiny envelope from the bag. Not a single person had written anything on the valentine but his or her own name. The words pre-printed on the cards sounded all sweet and romantic, but didn't mean a thing—*Valentine, will you be mine?*—since everyone knew the same message was sent to every single person in the class.

Kiley crumpled up the bag of valentines and pitched it across the room.

She fell backwards onto the carpeting, chewing furiously on the gum, and thought about her sister. Lucky Ginger. She had a boyfriend, even if Hunter was kind of dopey, in a puppy dog kind of way. He did have a cool name. *Hunter.* And Ginger sure got some great Valentine presents.

Then Kiley thought about the boys she knew in the fifth grade.

There was Josh, of course, practically like a pesky brother. She had known him since they were both in strollers.

There were those other boys she had thought about

inviting to join her new club... Marco and Dave and...T.J. T.J.

Kiley sat up suddenly. *Hey, what about T.J.?* she thought with a jolt. He sometimes got in trouble at school, but she had worked with him on a colonial village project in class, and he had been kind of nice.

He was sort of cute—tall, and he had that longish hair.

He did have a cool name. Better than Hunter.

Hmm, thought Kiley. *T.J. Hmmm...*

CHAPTER 4

T.J. Mariani, Known Troublemaker

Tell-All Question 30: What one thing about you would surprise people if they found out about it?

T.J. scowled as he pulled two crumpled notes from his backpack and threw them on the kitchen table. The first note, the one on white paper, came from that girl in his class, Kiley. Something about a club she was starting, and did he want to be part of it. *Sure*, thought T.J. *I'll be in Kiley's club. Why not?*

The second note, though, made him mad. He pushed his long hair back from his forehead and stared at the crumpled blue sheet. Everyone in the whole fifth grade had gotten the same note that morning. And they had all acted like they had just won some big prize from a radio station or the lottery or something.

"Cool," Josh, a kid who sat at his table in Mr. Garcia's class, had said. "This is going to be so awesome."

Kiley had even squealed so loud it hurt T.J.'s ears. "Oh, man, we are sooo lucky! I hope Anne and I get assigned to the same cabin! It will be like a long, long sleepover!"

Usually at lunchtime recess, the guys played basketball outside, and T.J. could almost always count on sinking the most shots and coming back from the chill air into the warm school all revved up. Today, though, it had been different. Today at lunch recess the guys had just stood around talking about that note. No one had even touched a basketball.

But T.J. thought the whole thing stunk. Big time.

Who was the genius who thought the entire fifth-grade class should leave Illinois and go to some Camp Kindred Spirits in Wisconsin this year and stay for four days? The school had never done anything like this before. So why start this year? With this class?

"Outdoor Education," they called it. "A chance to enjoy an out-of-classroom learning experience for four days," the note said. But four days meant something else. It meant three nights. Three nights sleeping in some group cabin. Away from home.

T.J. slumped down at the kitchen table in front of the two crumpled notes and sighed.

"What have you got there?" his grandmother asked, coming into the room with a basket of sweet-smelling laundry. "T.J., nothing bad happened today, did it? You didn't get another detention?"

T.J. handed her the camp note. "I'm not going," he announced.

His grandmother set down the laundry basket, reached for the rumpled blue sheet, and scanned the note.

"Ahhhh..." she began.

"I'm not going," T.J. repeated.

"Don't jump to a decision yet," said his grandmother gently. "Let's think about this. Let's talk about this."

T.J. shrugged, grabbed his backpack, and headed to his room.

What was there to think about? What was there to talk about?

Twice he had stayed somewhere overnight, somewhere away from home.

And twice something terrible had happened. Not to him, exactly, but...

It had made him vow never to sleep overnight away from home again.

He wasn't going to the fifth-grade camp.

And that was that.

CHAPTER 5

Josh's Scent of Trouble

Tell-All Question 30: What food makes you want to gag?

Josh pushed through the front door of his house, clutching the two notes—the white one and blue one—he'd been given at school that day. An unbelievable aroma floated out from the kitchen, so good it made Josh's mouth water. But then his face fell and his stomach twisted. He knew what that heavenly smell meant. Josh's mother was baking pies. Again.

His mom baked pies a lot. And, funny thing, all her pies seemed to end up in the homes of the families with a kid that Steve-O had been bullying.

Oh, his mom never came out and said, "I'm so sorry my boy shoved your son into the brick wall. Please don't be mad at our whole family. Here, have a peach pie." No, she always found some other reason to bring her freshly baked treats to a neighbor's door. Josh had overheard her a few times as he waited in the car.

"Mrs. Lovett, you did such a great job helping out with the school ice-cream social," she'd say. "This is just my way of thanking you for all you do for our kids."

Or she'd praise someone's work on the yearbook.

Or with the Scouts.

Or anything she could think of. But Josh recognized all those pies for what they were: peace offerings.

Steve-O loved pie. And Josh knew the fact that all those pies were heading out the door made Steve-O mad. But Steve-O was mad a lot, at other things, too.

Mrs. Bendle didn't get angry easily, and neither did Mr. Bendle. Yet somehow, Steve-O's temper was turned up like three notches higher than on your average kid.

So Mrs. Bendle baked a lot of pies.

For a moment, Josh wondered what had happened with Steve-O today. *Probably got himself another detention*, Josh thought. But then he decided he didn't want to ask. He didn't want to know. Instead, Josh handed his mom the blue note, the note that spelled out the best news Josh had heard in a long time. The news about Camp Kindred Spirits.

At first, Mrs. Bendle laughed. "Another note covered with your doodles, I see," she observed. Hand-sketched stars and swords, dragons and monsters fell, shot, galloped, and flung themselves down the borders and all along the back of the note. Josh grinned sheepishly. He always seemed to do that, draw all over the papers that were sent home.

"Hey, this sounds exciting!" his mom said, looking up from the note. "You'll be staying in cabins and going sledding and hiking and..."

Steve-O lumbered into the room just then.

"Is that about the camp?" Steve-O asked. "The fifth-grade camp? No fair! They didn't have camp when I was in fifth grade."

"It probably because of you that they *didn't* start it up last year," Josh shot back.

Steve-O narrowed his eyes.

"What's that other note you have there?" his mother asked quickly, changing the subject.

Josh almost forgot about the other note.

The note that had nearly spoiled his day, nearly quenched all his excitement for the fifth-grade camp program.

"Nothing," Josh answered. "Just some note from some other kid."

He shoved the white paper in his back pocket. The note from Kiley. About her club. Josh shivered.

What a really, really terrible idea for a club: The Tell-All Club.

CHAPTER 6

Anne's Revenge

Tell-All Question 45: What is something you do really, really well?

In the late afternoon, Anne heard the doorbell echoing down the hall. She flicked open the blinds of her bedroom window. *Josh's mom?* That was a surprise.

Mrs. Bendle stood alone on the front porch, holding something covered in aluminum foil. Steam, in wispy fingers, rose from around the foil's edges.

Anne heard her mother open the door, heard her greet Mrs. Bendle in an unusually cold voice.

What's up with her? Anne wondered.

She was curious.

She left the window, left her room, and stood in the hall, just out of sight of the two mothers.

"...And I just wanted to say a little thank-you for all the work you did last week at the school book fair. I hope you like pecan pie."

Mrs. Bendle's voice sounds way too happy, Anne thought. Almost chirpy. Anne heard the crinkling of foil, and knew Mrs. Bendle must be lifting a corner to show the pie.

"Thank you, Gerry," Anne's mom replied. "We do like pecan pie. Would you like to come in?"

"Oh," said Mrs. Bendle, sounding almost startled. "Oh, no, Diane. I need to get going…"

"Well, ah, Gerry," Anne heard her mother pause, then begin tentatively. "About your son…"

"Yes," said Mrs. Bendle quickly. "I guess my Josh and your Anne are good pals…"

"Not… *that* son," Anne's mom interrupted. "Your *Steven.* You must know by now. The principal said she'd call you today about the incident. Steve-O—er, Steven—took my son Alan's science and technology fair project and…well, he sat on it."

Anne gasped.

She didn't wait to hear the rest of their conversation. She ran down the hall to her little brother's room. "Alan," she whispered through the door. "Can I come in?"

She heard a soft sniffle from behind the door.

"Alan," she said. "I'm coming in now." She swung open the door.

Little Alan sat on the floor, next to a pile of wooden pieces and splinters. He squinted out of big, puffy, tear-filled eyes.

"Oh, Alan. Your bridge!"

"He sat on it!" Alan yelled. "That stupid Steve-O Bendle sat on it, 'cause I set it on a chair in the school hallway. He said he didn't see it, but he did. He did!"

Anne dropped to the floor and put her arm around her little brother.

She knew how much the science and technology fair meant to him. She herself had had trouble fitting into the new neighborhood since the move. It had been even harder for Alan, now a third-grade whiz kid, to fit in.

That Bendle family, thought Anne. Josh's words, those words he had screamed out last week, that he could hardly stand her, still stung. And now this.

That Bendle family is rotten to the core. Every one of them including Josh. Especially Josh.

"Oh, Alan," Anne said. "I'll help you any way I can. We can build another one."

But as she carefully sifted through the broken pieces, she was thinking about her anger at the Bendles, and the note Kiley had passed to her today, about the Tell-All Club.

If Kiley wants me to be in her club, Anne vowed to herself, *she better not let Josh Bendle join. I won't have anything to do with ANY Bendle anymore.*

When Alan's sniffling had slowed, Anne left his room. Some hazy plan began to form in her mind. She walked past the kitchen and the lingering scent of the fresh-baked pecan pie. She grabbed her coat. She grabbed her pink scarf. She began to walk.

Anne walked out her front door, through the cold and snow toward the Bendle house. She didn't know what she would do yet. What she would say. Something.

She rounded a corner. Down the street, she saw Josh in his driveway.

She watched Josh throw a basketball toward the basket on his garage. Missed.

He threw again. Missed.

Anne grew closer.

Josh threw again. Missed.

Anne reached Josh's driveway.

She had made her decision. She knew what she would do, how she'd get even. She didn't say a thing.

Anne grabbed the ball out of a startled Josh's hands.

She threw the ball. It swished through the net.

She stepped back, threw it again, and sunk it.

Anne did it again and again and again, moving herself to different positions, all over the driveway. She never missed. Not once.

Then she picked up the rebounding ball, threw it at Josh, and turned away without a word.

Anne heard the ball hit the pavement. Josh hadn't even been able to catch it, had fumbled with it and dropped it, of course.

Anne smiled under her big pink scarf, fluffed her gorgeous dark hair, and walked back toward home.

So there, stinky Josh Bendle.

So there.

CHAPTER 7

Kiley's Big Idea

Tell-All Question 49: Why do you want to join the Tell-All Club?

Kiley looked in the mirror and sighed.

Unfair, unfair, unfair.

"So how do you like it?" asked the purple-haired stylist between chomps on her bubblegum.

Kiley's mom ducked her head next to her daughter's and peered into the mirror.

"It's adorable!" gushed her mom. "Kiley, that style is so very attractive on you."

Kiley saw her blond hair cut in long wisps, softly framing her face.

But Kiley also saw the reflection of the two of them, mom and daughter, faces side by side.

She saw the purple-headed stylist look, too, and saw her expression.

Kiley knew the difference between her and her mother was surprising. Their coloring was identical, but otherwise they looked nothing alike. Kiley's mom was beautiful, like a model. Kiley knew this, not just because of what she could see herself, but because she heard people say it. Everywhere. In stores and at movie theaters she saw heads turn. At school, she heard it all the time— Oh, Kiley, your mom is so pretty."

And her mom *was* pretty. Not flashy pretty, but old-fashioned gorgeous, like Reese Witherspoon, maybe, only older. Kiley knew her own face was perfectly normal, kind of round with an average nose and mouth, and regular-type eyes. Not bad. A lot like her dad, in fact. But she wasn't drop-dead gorgeous.

Sometimes it could be tough, being the daughter of someone so beautiful.

It was even worse to be the little sister of someone just as beautiful. Someone like Ginger.

In fact, Kiley had chosen a haircut exactly like Ginger's current style. It looked fine. It just didn't look the way it did on Ginger.

"Let's go," said Kiley. She hopped out of the stylist's chair.

In the car on the way home, Kiley saw her mom glance back at her in the rearview mirror a couple of times. Mom looked worried.

"Don't you like your new cut?" Mom finally asked.

"It's fine," said Kiley. The haircut had been a

disappointment, though. It hadn't been the big change she'd hoped for. Sometimes she wished she had long, black, silky hair like lucky Anne Park.

But then Kiley decided not to think about her hair. Or her looks. Instead she wound her thoughts around the Tell-All Club.

She knew lots of kids would want to be in her Tell-All Club. She had tons of friends, much more than dumb old Ginger did.

And there was T.J., cute T.J. who always won the first-place ribbons at the school's Field Day.

He probably likes me. She thought about T.J. a moment, how his brown hair flew when he streaked down the field, or bounded in the air to make a basket.

Yeah, lots of people like me, Kiley silently told herself. *So see, being beautiful isn't everything.*

Back at home, Kiley asked, "Can I go on the computer for awhile?"

"It's getting late. Homework all done?" her mom asked.

"Yeah."

"Okay, then. Are you writing a story?"

"No," Kiley said. "Just...something. For my friends."

→|

Kiley slipped into the kitchen. She sat down at the tiny kitchen desk, turned on the family's laptop, and opened a new document: The Tell-All Club. She typed, pecking away with two fingers.

This is the Tell-All Club. To be in this very special club, you must be in fifth grade. You must also share your secrets by answering all these questions.

Question 1: Who do you like? (**REALLY** like, not just as a friend kind of like)

Kiley smiled. That was what she really wanted to know. She would email this and other questions to everyone she invited in the club—and give T.J. a printed copy since she didn't have his email address yet. But it was T.J.'s answer to this one question that really interested her.

Kiley looked at the screen again. *I probably shouldn't make that the very first question*, she thought. *Too obvious.* So she deleted it, and started again.

But what else should she ask?

She stared at the screen.

Ginger breezed into the kitchen then, home late after an evening's dance practice.

Ginger opened the fridge and grabbed the bowl of salad left over from dinner.

"Mom," Ginger yelled, pushing back her stylish, honey-colored hair. "Are we all out of my lo-cal ranch dressing?"

Kiley thought a moment.

Then she began typing.

Question 1: What is your favorite salad dressing?

CHAPTER 8

T.J.'s Tell-All Tricks

Tell-All Question 42: Have you ever been in trouble at school?

Detention, thought T.J. *How totally stupid.* He hadn't done anything wrong, not really. Not bad enough, anyway, to be kept after school in the learning center for a whole hour.

T.J. laid his head on the desk. He and that sixth-grade bully, Steve-O, were the only two kids there today. Steve-O probably deserved detention. He had probably done something awful.

But I didn't, T.J. thought. He knew some of his classmates had him figured as one of the wilder kids, someone who got his kicks out of breaking rules. But that wasn't true. Actually, each time T.J. got in trouble it *embarrassed* him. Sometimes, in fact, he had all he could do to keep from crying.

T.J. sighed, reached for his backpack, and pulled
out the big crumpled envelope Kiley had handed him
today. In black letters, the words "The Tell-All Club"
were printed on front. *I guess I can get this done now*, he
thought. He pulled out the sheets stapled together inside
the envelope.

**This is the Tell-All Club. To be in this very special club,
you must be in fifth grade. You must also share your secrets
by answering all these questions.**

Question 1: What is your favorite salad dressing?

Wish test questions were this easy, T.J. thought. He
wrote down "Italian." Then he stopped, scribbled it out,
and wrote, "I just let my salads go naked." He laughed
out loud, and Ms. Lentz, the teacher on guard, shot him
a look.

He scanned the rest of the questions, about favorite
colors, favorite pizza toppings, favorite television shows.
T.J. figured he could find some dumb answer for all of
Kiley's dumb questions.

For favorite color, he put "Green – the color of
money."

For favorite television show, he wrote, "I think the
commercials are WAY better than the shows."

He zipped down the list of questions until he got to
the last one.

**Question 50: Who do you like? (REALLY like, not just as a
friend kind of like)**

The answer he came up with for that one got him laughing so loud that Ms. Lentz marched over, made him put the stapled sheets back in the envelope, and told him to start reading the book *Hatchet* that he'd also brought along.

Steve-O snickered. Automatically, T.J. glanced at him. Steve-O screwed his face into a horrible expression, then half laughed, half snorted when T.J. flinched.

"Fifth-grade loser," Steve-O growled, too low for the teacher to hear.

Finally, after doing his time, T.J. let the school's front door bang behind him, then zipped his jacket up against the cold.

He still couldn't believe he'd gotten detention for some-thing so stupid, and he still felt angry.

He kicked at the snow under his feet, as if it were the snow's fault.

Why, he wondered, *do I always get busted for some little thing that somebody decides to make a big deal about?*

It had happened today, during lunch. He'd picked up a pile of snow, packed it into a ball, and tossed it through the basketball hoop. So big deal, right?

Except the week before, some little kindergarten boy had gotten a snowball in the face from his own second-grade sister. The little boy's face had been cut by a piece of gravel in the snowball. So then the principal, Dr. Wu, started squawking during the morning announcements that there was a zero tolerance policy about snowballs:

Anyone seen throwing a snowball would receive an automatic detention.

But, T.J. thought, *shouldn't that mean throwing a snowball AT someone?*

So some lunch lady saw him make the snowball and toss it through the hoop, and she ran over, and suddenly everyone was treating him like some kind of criminal.

And that second-grade girl who started the whole thing by smashing snow in her brother's face? No one bothered handing her a detention. She probably walked away with no punishment at all.

Figures, thought T.J. He rounded the corner of the school on his way home, and froze in his steps.

Great. There was Josh Bendle. One of the "good" kids, whom teachers loved and who never got in trouble. One of the perfect kids who thought the fifth-grade camp was going to be the greatest thing since video games. T.J. wondered if Josh knew about the detention. Maybe he didn't. After all, hadn't Josh been at a yearbook staff meeting at lunch today, when the whole thing went down?

T.J. hoped Josh wouldn't ask why he was at school this late. He didn't need *that* humiliation today.

But Josh didn't notice him at first. T.J. stopped, leaned his lanky frame against the brick wall of the school, and watched.

Josh stood on the school's deserted basketball court, aiming a ball at the net. Little wisps of snow blew on the wind and circled around the court.

It's freezing today, thought T.J. *What's Josh doing out here by himself?*

Josh sent the ball flying. It hit the backboard, then rebounded off.

When Josh turned to get the ball, he saw T.J.

T.J. was surprised to see that Josh looked embarrassed himself.

"Hey," Josh said, and nodded.

"Hey," T.J. answered. "What're you doing?"

"Oh," Josh answered. "Just, you know..."

"Don't you have a net at home, on your garage? I think I've seen you out there."

"Yeah," Josh answered. "I used to shoot there. Don't really like shooting there anymore."

T.J. stayed silent for a moment. Josh did, too. *He's not going to ask me why* I'm *here*, T.J. thought with relief.

"You know, I think I can help you with your game," T.J. said. "It's not like I'm an expert or anything, but I've been on my church team and I play at the Y, and I've had a lot of coaches give me some pointers."

"Yeah?" said Josh, and he shrugged. "Sure, if you want to."

"Well, do you want to walk to my house, and shoot baskets there?" T.J. asked. "I live just down the street. And you know, my grandmother's expecting me, and if I don't show up, she'll send out a search party."

Josh laughed. T.J. did, too. Suddenly T.J. kind of

liked the idea of having one of the "good" kids to hang out with. And besides, Josh could sure use some help on his game.

"Plus," T.J. continued, warming up to the idea, "If we go to my house, I can talk my gram into making us hot chocolate, and maybe she'll throw some of those big hot pretzels in the oven, too. You can call your mom from my house to let her know you're there."

"Yeah," said Josh, "but I can ask her now."

"Call on your cell?" T.J. asked.

"Nah. She's right here." Josh nodded toward a car pulling into the parking lot. "She's picking up my brother—the jerk snagged himself another detention today. Can you believe it?"

T.J.'s face reddened at the mention of detention. He turned to see the car as it halted in front of the school, and saw Steve-O walk toward it and get in.

"Steve-O is your brother?"

"Yeah," said Josh. "Didn't you know that?"

"No," said T.J. "I mean, you two are never together, you don't hang out with each other or anything. And, like, you're total opposites. So, no, I had no idea."

CHAPTER 9

Josh Tells All, Too

Tell-All Question 12: What was your most embarassing moment?

Josh felt queasy as he gripped the phone and listened to Kiley rattle off her instructions. "I've sent everyone an email—well, everyone but T.J., 'cause it turns out he doesn't have a computer, so I just printed it out and handed it to him at school—anyway, I've sent everyone an email with all these questions you have to answer to be in the club."

"What kind of questions?"

"Personal questions. This is called the Tell-All Club, Josh. Anyway, just copy the message into a reply, answer each one, and send it off. Simple."

"Okay."

"And Josh, do it right now."

Then she hung up.

Good old bossy Kiley, thought Josh. She had been like that since they both were three. He remembered her sitting in his sandbox, telling him she would take the yellow pail and the sifter, and he'd have to play with the green pail and the broken shovel. But he liked her anyway. That's just how she was. Now, though, Kiley had this new group of friends. And he wasn't sure how he felt about them—Marco and Miranda and T.J.

But T.J., he thought, *seemed kind of cool.* When he had gone to his house after school today, T.J. had taught him how to center himself before letting a ball fly. Josh had actually made a few baskets, right in a row, and from some distance. Then they had gone inside for hot chocolate, hot pretzels and some video games. And T.J. had shown him his pet rat. Leave it to T.J. to have such a cool pet.

But there was someone else who'd be in the club. Anne Park. She used to be his friend, sort of. Then, like Kiley, Anne started hanging out with all the popular kids. Kiley and Anne were good friends now, too, and Anne would definitely be in the Tell-All Club.

Josh felt funny about Anne, though. Judging from that strange thing that happened in his driveway when Anne had swiped the basketball and showed off like she did, well, Anne must really hate him.

Then he had almost freaked out when, earlier today, Anne had come walking down the street as he and T.J. shot baskets. *Geez*, he had thought, *is she going to grab the ball and make a fool of me again? In front of T.J.?* Quickly, Josh had told T.J. "Ready to go inside now?" And so they had.

Still, Josh liked to belong, be a part of the group. And, despite everything, he did want to be in Kiley's club. He went to the computer in the study and clicked it on. Sure enough, Kiley had sent an email.

Reluctantly, he pulled it up, and looked over the form that popped up.

It was awful.

Suddenly his stomach went from queasy to aching. To begin with, the directions were totally unclear.

This is the Tell-All Club. To be in this very special club, you must be in fifth grade. You must also share your secrets by answering all these questions.

What exactly did that mean? Did you have to answer everything "right" to be allowed in the club? Would the answers be, well—*judged*?

Josh wondered how the popular kids, like T.J., would answer each question. T.J. would know what to write, his answers would all be totally cool.

And what would Kiley do with all this info? That was the scariest thing of all.

Josh took a deep breath.

Please, just don't let me make a fool of myself, he silently wished.

Then he read the first question.

Question 1: What is your favorite salad dressing?

Josh wondered if there was a good way to answer that question. He liked French dressing—but it was sweet, and red and, well...*French*. Was that not tough guy enough?

He was sure blue cheese would be a wrong answer. If you liked blue cheese, you'd be teased for liking something smelly, something only your strange Uncle Henry liked. Josh sighed. Compared to these questions, the math test he had taken today was a breeze. He finally settled on Italian dressing. T.J. was part Italian, judging from his last name anyway—Mariani. Maybe Italian dressing is what T.J. would choose, too.

Josh went on through the questions, stumbling along with answers as best he could.

Question 2: What is your favorite T.V. show?

He typed in name of the latest reality show he heard some kids talking about at school. He'd only actually seen one episode himself, and he thought it was a little dumb, but it was a safe answer.

Question 3: What is your favorite color?

He typed in "blue", figuring no one could tease him about that. Josh continued through the questions, answering each one carefully. Then he paused.

Question 7: What is your favorite memory?

The favorite memory question made Josh smile. Without much thought, he started typing the story of the time he found the little kid crying her eyes out in a store. She was lost, and the mom was nowhere in sight, so he had walked the kid to a clerk. But the sobbing little kid—she was probably four years old—had refused to go with the clerk and had grabbed hold of Josh's hand. So Josh and the girl followed the clerk to an intercom phone, and the clerk had made an announcement about a lost little girl in a yellow sundress. Then a worried looking woman had come rushing up. First she hugged the girl, then she hugged Josh and thanked him over and over. She had even called him a hero.

When Josh was done typing his little story, he nodded to himself. He worked a long time on all the other, agonizing questions. Then Josh faced the final question.

He stared at it.

Question 50: Who do you like? (REALLY like, not just as a friend kind of like)

Josh felt himself break into a cold sweat. He knew what the question meant—who would you want to be your, like, girlfriend. *But I don't like any girl*, he thought. *Well, not that way. Geez, what's wrong with me? I probably should like someone.*

Josh picked up a pencil and began chewing on it furiously. Would he get away with typing in "NO ONE." Nah. He'd probably get disqualified from the club, or something. How about something safe, like a movie star? Or what about that sixth-grader on the yearbook staff, Nori Anders? Everyone thought Nori was cute. But if anyone told Nori he liked her (which he didn't really—he only thought she was cute, like someone you might see on a commercial) he'd just die. Josh's hands were sweaty. His stomach hurt even more.

He felt awash in worry, when something else began pricking at him. That favorite memory question. His answer had been way too stupid. Why had he put down that the lady called him a hero? He hadn't really done anything. It would seem like he was bragging over nothing. He was just about to scroll back up the screen and delete the answer.

Then he heard clumping behind him.

Steve-O pushed him aside. "My turn at the computer, chump," his big brother announced. Before Josh could stop him, Steve-O bent toward the screen and read the question—the last question:

Who do you like? (**REALLY** like, not just as a friend kind of like)

Steve-O let out a terrible half laugh, half snort. Josh grabbed his arm, but he couldn't budge the big lug. Steve-O flicked him off like a fly and began pecking at the keyboard.

Then to his horror, Josh caught sight of the screen. Steve-O had typed in an answer to the last question.

He wrote: ANNIE POO.

"NOOOOOOOO!" Josh screamed. Steve-O looked over his shoulder and gave Josh an evil grin. Josh knocked Steve-O's hand aside, grabbed the keyboard, and began backspacing over the word, deleting the last letters one by one. Josh managed to delete the last two O's before Steve-O got the keyboard back. Over Steve-O's shoulder, Josh could just see the monitor—he could just see that the answer on the glowing screen now read: *Annie P.*

Steve-O directed the cursor to send, and clicked the mouse.

CHAPTER 10

Anne Tells Too Much

Tell-All Question 17: What is the dumbest thing you've ever done?

Anne hated how, when she was mad, her thoughts just circled around and around in her brain like a puppy chasing its tail. No matter how hard she tried to concentrate on something else, the thing that was making her mad seemed to shove everything else aside and say, "No, me, me, me! You have to give me all your attention!"

And now, before dinner, while she was supposed to be studying her spelling words, she couldn't stop thinking about Josh Bendle.

Not only because of the "I can hardly stand her" incident.

Not only because his brother Steve-O smashed Alan's project.

Not only because Mrs. Bendle thought she could make everything all better with a pecan pie.

She was mad about something new, something that had happened today.

Josh, her once good friend, had totally snubbed her. And worse, it had happened in front of somebody else.

Anne had been ready to apologize to Josh for the whole grabbing-the-basketball incident. She wanted to be friends again. It had been a bit snotty, what she had done.

Anne even walked to Josh's house in the cold after school to try to talk to him. Mrs. Bendle told her Josh was at T.J.'s house. That had surprised Anne. The two had never been friends, not as far as she could tell. But Anne knew where T.J. lived. Despite the chilling temperatures, she wrapped her pink scarf around her face, and hiked on over to T.J.'s house. She saw T.J. and Josh shooting baskets together, but as she drew nearer Josh gave her a funny look. Anne felt a coldness that did not come from the icy wind. And she felt most unwelcome.

Josh immediately stopped shooting, grabbed the ball, and held tight.

"We're going inside now," Josh announced. Then the two jumped to the porch, pulled open the door, and left Anne standing there. By herself. Alone. In the cold.

She had stomped home totally fuming, her pink scarf flying behind her.

Anne hadn't been able to concentrate on anything else that day.

Now, still angry, she flung her spelling words aside, went to the study, and crashed down on the computer chair.

She pulled up the dumb Tell-All Club questionnaire. Kiley had nagged her all day, telling her she must fill it out tonight.

Fine, thought Anne, *I'll fill it out.*

She didn't care how anyone else had answered the questions. She knew what she wanted to say.

She snorted at the first, salad dressing question. She typed: **Any salad dressing JOSH BENDLE doesn't like.**

For the favorite T.V. show question, she typed in: **I watch professional basketball. Because I can actually sink a ball, unlike JOSH BENDLE.**

When she read, **What is your favorite memory?** she smiled. **Watching JOSH BENDLE'S face when I stole the ball from him and sank basket after basket after basket,** she typed.

She flew through the rest of the questions, answering them all the same way. Then she came to the final question.

Question 50: Who do you like? (REALLY like, not just as a friend kind of like)

Anne's fingers trembled as she hit the Caps Lock key and typed: **NO ONE. BUT I CAN'T STAND ANYONE WITH THE LAST NAME BENDLE.**

Fiercely, she clicked on Send.

Anne sat for a moment, letting out a deep sigh. She

stretched her legs out, crossed her arms, and slumped down in the chair. She waited to feel good, to feel a rush from getting back at that stupid Josh Bendle.

No good feeling came.

Instead, she felt rotten.

Then she gasped.

A cold chill tickled her back.

She began to shiver.

"What was I thinking?" she cried aloud.

She grabbed the computer monitor between her hands.

"Oh, no…now what stupid, stupid thing have I done?"

Then she sprinted for the phone.

CHAPTER 11

Kiley Awaits Answers

Tell-All Question 1: What is your favorite salad dressing?

Kiley sat at the dining room table, her feet swinging back and forth impatiently. *C'mon, c'mon*, she thought. *Let's get this over with.*

Earlier that day, her mother had said they were having company for dinner.

"Grandma?" Kiley had guessed. "Uncle Jack and Aunt Rose?"

"No," her mother had answered. "Hunter is having dinner with us."

"Hunter is NOT company," Kiley had protested.

Now he sat directly across from her, spooning pot roast and vegetables onto his plate. Ginger sat next to him, all moony-eyed.

Kiley pushed the pot roast around her plate. She was dying to read the Tell-All Club answers. Both Anne and Josh had promised to email them tonight, and she hadn't had a chance to go to the computer yet. But it wasn't *their* answers that she really cared about.

Just before dinner, a knock had sounded as they were all saying grace. Mom had excused herself and answered the door. It was T.J.

Kiley jumped up.

"Sit down, young lady," her father had instructed. "Your mother will speak to the visitor."

Kiley scowled. "But…" she began. T.J. had never, ever been at her door before.

"Sit down," her father had repeated.

Kiley slumped back into her seat.

What's going on? she thought. *We aren't usually this…this…formal at dinner.*

But the answer was sitting directly across from her, with a stupid grin on his face. It was all because of the "company." Ginger's boyfriend. Hunter.

Because of him, Mom and Dad were pretending to be so prim and proper. Heck, they had even put out the fancy salad dressing server, the one that offered three choices of dressing in little silver cups. *That thing only comes out at Christmas dinner*, Kiley noted.

Kiley craned her neck to try to catch a glimpse of T.J. All she could see from her seat in the dining room was Mom's back and a bit of T.J.'s lanky frame.

Then the door closed and her mother returned with a crumpled brown envelope. She set it on the living room coffee table and returned to the dining room.

Kiley could see the envelope from where she sat.

Kiley began stirring the vegetables on her plate with a spoon.

"Kiley…" Dad began to chide her about her manners. Then the phone rang.

Dad sighed, excused himself, and went to pick it up.

"Hi there, Josh," she heard him say. "No, Kiley can't talk right now. Yes, I'm sure it is important. She'll talk to you tomorrow."

"Daaaaad…" Kiley protested.

But her father gave her a look. "Josh, I have to go. There's a call on the other line. Good-bye." Dad clicked the receiver. "Hello. Oh hi, Anne. No, Kiley's not available. We have company tonight. Urgent, you say? Well, she'll call you tomorrow."

"Hey!" Kiley yelped.

"Shhh," Mom warned.

"Guess what!" Ginger suddenly chirped. "I asked Hunter to the turn-about dance. And he said yes!"

Kiley watched her father put the phone down. She groaned.

"What's a turn-about dance?" her mother asked.

"That's when girls have to ask the guys out," said Ginger. "And you won't believe how I asked this guy!" She gave Hunter a sidelong glance and a nudge with her elbow.

51

Hunter blushed.

"How did you ask this guy?" her father asked, returning to his seat.

Ginger grinned. "I took sidewalk chalk, and wrote it in giant letters across his driveway, so the whole neighborhood could see it. I wrote: 'Hunter, I'm crazy about you. Will you go to the dance with me?'"

Kiley sat up straight, interested.

Dad started coughing loudly.

"Ginger, you did?" asked her mother, looking slightly shocked.

"Yeah," Hunter grunted. "It was cool."

Yeah, thought Kiley. *That* IS *kind of cool.*

CHAPTER 12

T.J.'s Courageous Answer

Tell-All Question 47: What is the bravest thing you've ever done?

"Honey, can I talk to you?"

T.J. stiffened when he saw what his grandmother held. He threw aside the anime book he was reading.

"Sure, Gram. What is it?"

His grandmother sat on the edge of his bed and smoothed out a piece of paper.

"I found this in the trash," she said. "The Fifth-Grade Camp Kindred Spirits permission slip."

"Yeah," T.J. said. "Figured since I'm not going, there was no sense giving it to you."

His grandma looked at him.

"T.J.," she began. "I think you need to do this."

T.J. didn't answer.

"T.J., it's time."

T.J. turned away from his grandmother and stretched out across his bed.

"T.J.," she said. "You can go. Nothing bad will happen."

"How do you know?" he said. He could feel himself starting to cry. He hated crying, even in front of his grandmother.

"It happened twice," he said.

His grandmother sighed.

"Yes," she said. "It might seem that way, but…"

"I don't want to talk about it," T.J. said.

"You went to stay with your cousins a few days and…"

"Gram…"

"You went to stay with your cousins a few days, and when you came home, your dad was gone. And you found out your parents were getting a divorce."

T.J. hadn't seen his dad much since.

"Please…" said T.J.

"And then, years later, you came to stay with me for the week while your mom went on a business trip, and there was the accident…"

T.J. put his hands over his ears.

Gently, his grandmother pulled his hands away. "I know you're afraid, T.J. I know you're afraid that if you go away from home, you'll lose…someone else."

T.J. buried his face in his pillow.

"But you have a whole life ahead of you. And someday, you'll want to go away, have to go away...on the eighth-grade trip to Springfield, on your high school trip to Washington, D.C., and then to college. And this is the first step. You should go. Don't hang around here with some old lady while all your friends are off having fun. Your new friend, Josh, he's going, isn't he?"

"He can't wait," T.J. answered, his face still in the pillow.

"See?" his grandmother said. "You know you'll have fun. You will. And everything here will be just fine. I promise."

"Your mother," his grandma continued, very softly. "She loved new experiences. She loved camping. Your mother would have wanted you to go. She always dreamed you'd have a full, exciting life."

His grandmother paused. "Will you think about it?" she asked.

T.J. felt tears spilling, spilling onto the pillow.

"T.J., will you promise me that you'll at least think about it? For me?"

Still, T.J. didn't lift his head. But with his face in his pillow, he gave his grandmother the slightest nod yes.

CHAPTER 13

Josh Gets Wise

Tell-All Question 37: What makes you laugh?

Josh had just let himself out of the house to head for school when he saw his next door neighbor Kiley.

Good, he thought. *I can talk to her about that Tell-All Club questionnaire, beg her not to show it to Anne.* But then he saw that Kiley was heading for him like a charging rhino.

"Who," Kiley demanded when she reached him, "is Katie?"

She's lost it, Josh thought. But he said "Katie?"

"Yes, Katie," said Kiley. "Is she some new girl, someone who has just moved in? Is she on the yearbook staff with you?"

"No," said Josh. "There's no one named Katie."

Kiley threw her backpack on the ground, unzipped

it, and ripped a paper out of a crumpled envelope.

"Question 50," she read. "'Who do you like?' And here's the answer: 'She's blond, she's cute, we like hanging out together. I know I'll never meet another girl like her. She stole my heart.'"

Kiley looked up. Josh just stared at her.

"That is T.J's answer to question 50," Kiley said. "I called him this morning."

"You called before school?"

"Why not? And I told him his answer didn't count. He had to fill in a name. And he said 'Okay, her name is Katie' and hung up."

"Oh," said Josh.

"So who's Katie? You hang out with T.J. You must know who his girlfriend is. So tell me," Kiley demanded.

"Kiley, I've been to his house once," Josh said. "And," he put in quickly, "About Anne...you didn't happen to show her..."

"Why won't you tell me who Katie is? What are you hiding from me?" Kiley crossed her arms.

Suddenly Josh grinned. "You like T.J., don't you?"

Kiley's eyes grew wide. "No way! I didn't say that!"

"Oh, okay," Josh said knowingly. Then he sighed. "Honestly, I don't know of any new girl named Katie. Maybe she's a sixth-grader or something. I don't know. But I need to tell you something about my Tell-All answers. Steve-O messed with them. You have to promise NOT to show them to Anne," Josh pleaded.

Kiley glared at him.

She's mad that I won't tell her who Katie is, Josh thought. *But I can't tell her what I don't know!*

"It's too late," Kiley snapped. "I forwarded your answers to her this morning." Kiley dived back into her backpack.

"And this might interest you," she said. "Here's Anne's questionnaire. I printed it out this morning."

And she flung three stapled papers at Josh.

Kiley turned and marched toward the school.

Josh stooped to pick up the sheets from where they landed in the snow.

He held them against his coat for moment.

He felt a kind of shock.

What would Anne think when she read what Steve-O wrote—that he liked her? And not just as a friend?

I'm going to die, he thought.

But what if, Josh suddenly hoped, what if Anne hasn't looked at her email yet this morning? Maybe he could talk to her first at school, explain.

Then he looked down at the sheets of Anne's Tell-All questionnaire, still pressed against his coat.

Did he feel right, reading her answers? Should Kiley really be passing all their answers back and forth like this? Weren't they kind of, you know, private?

Kiley's mad, he thought. *She's mad, and she's not thinking about what she's doing. She wants everyone to be as miserable as she is. All because of some mysterious girl named Katie.*

Then a little thought began to nibble at Josh. Katie. Katie. Why did that name sound familiar? Josh seemed to remember T.J. telling him something about a Katie yesterday.

And then Josh knew.

Of course T.J. liked Katie.

Katie was blond and sweet, Josh recalled.

T.J. was crazy about her, he had told Josh so himself.

And why not?

Katie was T.J.'s pet rat.

CHAPTER  *14*

Anne Gets a Shock

Tell-All Question 28: What's the best advice you ever gave someone?

Anne opened bleary eyes and looked at her alarm clock.

Nine o'clock! School had started half an hour ago!

"Mom!" she called, frantically jumping out of bed.

The motion made her forehead, her stomach and the back of her neck ache, and she sat back down on the edge of her bed. Anne began to shake.

Her mother appeared at the bedroom door.

"Get back in bed, honey," Mom said. "You're running a temperature. When I came in to wake you this morning, I felt your forehead and could tell you were feverish. So I let you sleep. And I'm not surprised you're sick. Your brother is home with a fever today, too."

Mom touched her cool hand to Anne's forehead.

"Let me get the thermometer," Mom said.

Anne's head felt heavy and her body stiff. But something else was bothering her. What was it? Her brain seemed too foggy to form any thoughts this morning.

But there was something...

And then she remembered. The Tell-All questionnaire. She was supposed to get up first thing this morning and call Kiley, and make her promise to delete all the nasty answers she had typed about Josh, make her promise not to say anything to anyone. But now, Kiley would already be at school for the day. In the same class as Josh. What if she told him about all the mean things Anne had written?

"Oh, no," Anne moaned. She stood up and dragged herself to the study and sat down at the computer. She must have been coming down with this flu bug last night, she realized. Maybe that explained why she had been so cranky. Maybe that's why she had acted so impulsively. But Anne could hardly remember how she answered all those questions. If she checked the Sent folder, she could reread her responses. Maybe, she hoped, maybe they weren't so bad.

But as she opened up the email program, she saw it. A message to her from Kiley. The subject line said: **Josh's Tell-All Answers.**

"Anne." She heard a soft voice call her name. She pulled her eyes away from the computer screen. Alan, wrapped in his little plaid robe, stood staring at her. He looked pale and weak. He looked like she felt.

"Anne, I have a plot."

Anne still felt like her brain had been wrapped in fuzzy cotton.

"A plot?" she echoed, stupidly.

"Yeah. I have a plan to get revenge on that bully Steve-O for sitting on my bridge."

"Oh, Alan," Anne said. "Don't. Take it from your big sister. Revenge is a very, very bad idea. It only makes things worse."

"But I want to tell you about my plan," Alan whispered. "Steve-O deserves it."

"There you two are," Mrs. Park said, appearing with the thermometer in one hand. "You should both be in bed," she scolded. "Now scoot." She gave Alan a small push toward his room.

"Mom, I just have to check one thing," pleaded Anne.

"Just one thing, then," Mom said. "But in the meantime," she stuck the electronic thermometer in Anne's mouth. "Keep it under your tongue. I'll be right back."

Anne turned back to the screen. She opened the message from Kiley. It said:

Anne, thought you might find this VERY interesting. Kiley

And there, below her note, were the Tell-All questions with all of Josh's answers. Anne froze. *Should I read these?* she wondered. For about half a second.

She couldn't help herself. Anne scrolled down

through the boring questions about salad dressing and favorite colors. Then she read the favorite memory. It was all about how Josh had helped some little girl lost in a store. Anne remembered how he had helped her, too, when she was a little girl lost in a new school, looking for the nurse's office.

He really is a nice guy, thought Anne. *And I have been so rotten to him.*

Then she scrolled down more, to the very last question, about who he really, really liked.

Anne was so surprised at his answer that her mouth fell open, and the thermometer dropped into her lap.

Who did Josh like?

Really, really like?

He liked her.

Annie P

CHAPTER 15

Kiley Gets Bold

Tell-All Question 46: What is the craziest thing you've ever done?

Kiley hugged the bucket of sidewalk chalk to her chest. The bushes she crouched behind scratched at her face. The driveway, she noted, was clear. No snow, no ice. T.J. himself had probably shoveled it a couple days ago after the last snowfall. The sun that had shown surprisingly warm that Thursday afternoon had melted away any bits that had been left.

Kiley crept out. From here, she could see the front windows of T.J.'s house. Only one dim light shone. She couldn't tell if anyone was home or not, but she hoped the gathering twilight would offer some cover.

Kiley reached into the bucket and grabbed a thick blue piece of chalk and moved forward. Then she bent down and scraped the chalk along the cement, at the top of the driveway near the garage door. The scraping sound seemed loud in the quiet evening. "T.J." she wrote. Cautiously, she moved down and wrote a second line, choosing green chalk this time. "I."

Next, Kiley drew a giant heart in pink, followed by a lavender "You."

She stepped back to inspect her work. "T.J. I ♥ You."

It looked good. *What a great way to let him, let the world know I like him*, she thought. It was sure to work. It had worked for Ginger.

Finally, with orange chalk, Kiley bent to write her name. As she scraped out a "K," she saw the headlights of a car come around the corner. Kiley froze. Then she bolted. She ran two houses down and dove into the front bushes.

And a good thing, too. The car headed straight for T.J.'s house and began to pull into the driveway. Then it stopped. The headlights remained on for what seemed like a long time. Kiley held her breath. What if it were T.J.? What would he think?

An older lady stepped out of the driver's side of the car. Kiley heard her laugh. "T.J.," the lady called out. "You have to see this!" Then another car door opened. This time, T.J. stepped out.

In the glow of the headlights, Kiley could see T.J. look down and read the writing. He crossed his arms, and when he turned his face to the older woman, Kiley could see from his profile that T.J. was smiling, though he did look a little embarrassed.

Mission accomplished, thought Kiley. *Even if I didn't get to write out my whole name…*

Kiley's thoughts suddenly ground to a horrifying halt.

I didn't write my whole name, thought Kiley. *I didn't get a chance. I only wrote K… for Kiley.*

She slapped her forehead.

Or, Kiley winced, *K… for Katie.*

CHAPTER *16*

T.J. Gets Busted

Tell-All Question 31: What is in your locker right now?

As T.J. pulled open the big school doors Friday
morning, he still felt exhilarated from the extra exertion
he had put in before his breakfast. Early that morning,
before the other kids would walk past his house on their
way to school, he had bundled up and gone out to the
driveway. He had started with an old stiff-straw broom,
and tried to sweep away the chalky letters. Then he had
made snowballs—which wasn't a big crime at his own
home like it was at school—and pelted them at the
remaining chalk smears in the driveway. He had gone
over everything one last time with the broom. It had
worked. Little remained, except a few bright smudges,
of the "T.J. I ♥ You" message that had appeared so
mysteriously last night.

The mystery, though, wasn't WHO had done it. He could figure *that* out easily enough. The reason was how—and why? Why was she acting so crazy?

Just thinking about it, as he sauntered to his locker, made his face grow warm. Maybe the energy he felt wasn't only about the extra work he had done this morning.

T.J. spun the combination on the locker's dial and popped open the door. He thought again that it was pretty great to have his own locker. Only the older grades—fifth and sixth—had them. The little kids had coat hooks at the back of their rooms for their stuff.

The hallway filled with kids coming in that morning. Out of the corner of his eye, he saw Kiley down the hall. She seemed to be watching him. She had a funny kind of look on her face. She looked like, at any moment, she might walk over and talk to him. T.J. felt a range of feelings—embarrassment was just one of them.

Then Anne walked by, a big pink scarf scrunched under her chin. T.J. didn't know Anne well. But he knew he didn't want to talk to Kiley that minute. It would be too weird. So he followed Anne and said quickly, "Hey, how's it going?"

Anne stopped, and turned surprised eyes toward him. "Fine," she said. "Or, at least better," she added. "You know I was out a couple days. Home with the flu. My brother, too. Today is our first day back."

T.J. nodded, not sure what to say. "Too bad," he

finally mumbled. "I mean, that you were sick."

Anne looked back at him. Her head was tilted. "You mind if I ask you a question, T.J.?"

T.J. shrugged.

"You filled out that Tell-All questionnaire for Kiley's club?"

T.J. nodded.

"Did she show you anyone else's answers?"

"No," said T.J.. "But I haven't talked to her much in the last couple of days."

"And has Josh said anything to you…about those questions? Or other people's answers?"

"Haven't talked to him in a while, either."

"Oh," said Anne. "Okay. Umm. I should go now."

"OK," said T.J. They both turned. And there stood Kiley. Just down the hall. Glaring at them.

T.J. watched Anne move toward her, but Kiley quickly turned her back and was gone. Anne took off after her.

And then a noise blasted down the hall from the other direction. A pound-pound-pounding that echoed off the walls. T.J. could see the back of Steve-O, his neck bright red, his fists smashing at his unopened locker door.

The teacher, Mr. Garcia, shot out of one of the classroom doors.

"Steven," Mr. Garcia said sternly. "Steven Bendle, stop!"

"It won't open," T.J. heard Steve-O yell. "Someone messed with it."

T.J. saw Mr. Garcia turn to inspect the locker, and T.J. turned back to his own, still open locker.

Hey, T.J. thought, as he looked down inside his locker. *What's that?* Something lay crumpled under his coat, near his boots. T.J. bent to pick it up. It was a tube of some kind. But as he stood up, he found the tube—a nearly empty tube of super glue—clung to his fingers.

"Hey!" he said aloud in his surprise. Even when he shook his hand, the tube stuck fast to his fingers.

"You!" he heard Steve-O yell. And suddenly, Steve-O was charging at him from down the hall.

T.J. felt Steve-O's hand clamp onto his shoulders. He felt Steve-O's breath in his face. "You're the idiot who glued my locker shut," Steve-O screamed, then he pushed him, full force. T.J. felt himself slam backwards into a locker. The locker handle struck painfully into his back.

Steve-O was clomping forward for another round, but now Mr. Garcia and Ms. Lentz had raced down the hall, and were pulling Steve-O back. Steve-O flared out with a last kick and grazed T.J.'s shin.

Mr. Garcia and Ms. Lentz each had Steve-O by an arm, and began hustling him in the direction of the principal's office.

"T.J., you come with us," Mr. Garcia called over his shoulder. "You have some explaining to do, too."

So T.J. slammed his locker closed with his foot, and with the tube of glue still hanging from his fingers, he followed.

Detention, T.J. thought. *Another stupid detention for something I didn't do.*

Back at home that night, T.J. wondered at the strange events of the day. He hadn't received a detention after all. Not yet anyway. The principal, Dr. Wu, had decided that first they would give him a chance to explain himself, explain how he could possibly be innocent of gluing Steve-O's locker closed with all the evidence stuck to his fingers.

And then Dr. Wu hinted that it might not be a detention this time, but some other punishment he must suffer.

T.J. might—if found guilty—have to miss the fifth-grade camp.

"After all," the principal said with a harrumph. "It's a privilege to go to the fifth-grade camp."

T.J. said nothing. As much as hated being blamed for something he didn't do, this would be a great out. Nobody would wonder why he hadn't gone to camp if they knew he wasn't allowed to go.

"Come in with your grandmother on Monday before school and we'll talk about this," Dr. Wu said.

Steve-O, though, really got in trouble. Once the

nurse saw the red marks on T.J.'s back and shin, Steve-O's mom got a call to take Steve-O home for the day.

The nurse had also managed to get the glue tube off T.J.'s finger, but some skin had peeled off in the process. His wrapped-up finger felt tender through the bandage, and he felt miserable.

Now, as the light outside grew dim, T.J. wandered to his bedroom, in need of a friend. As he leaned over Katie's cage, T.J. still felt a twinge where the locker handle had dug into his back. Gently, he picked up the rat. She nosed around his bandage for a moment. Then T.J. looked Katie straight into her fuzzy face. "It's been a rough day," he said to her.

He could tell she understood. The way she moved her little face to look in his eyes told him she understood.

A crunching noise sounded outside, in front of the house.

With Katie still cupped in his hand, T.J. crept to the window, figuring to catch a certain someone scraping another message in chalk along the driveway.

Instead, he saw a woman walking up to the porch. It was difficult to tell in the dark, but it looked like Josh's mom. He had only seen Mrs. Bendle a couple of times. She was Steve-O's mom, too, he reminded himself. And she had never been to his house before.

"What a weird day this has been," T.J. whispered to Katie.

The lady—Josh's mom—rang the doorbell, and T.J.

heard his grandmother head for the door. When the door opened, a bright shaft of light fell on Mrs. Bendle, and T.J. saw that she held something. Something in a pie tin, all warm and steamy and covered in foil.

CHAPTER 17

Complications for Josh

Tell-All Question 39: What drives you crazy?

Out of the corner of his eye, Josh saw Anne in the school hall Monday morning before class. Quickly, Josh dove into the boy's bathroom. He and Anne hadn't talked since Kiley had passed out all the Tell-All answers. Josh still couldn't believe Anne had written such nasty things. And it was doubly embarrassing now that Anne probably thought, from Steve-O's answer to Question 50, that Josh had some mad crush on her.

Josh peeked out the bathroom door, but then saw T.J. go by. He shot back inside. The whole thing with T.J was another big mess. How embarrassing to have your stupid brother pound on your newest friend. And then to have your mother scurry over with one of her pies. How could he face T.J. after that?

Finally, Josh edged his way out the door, and nearly bumped into Kiley.

"Arghhh," he moaned under his breath.

Yes, Kiley was an old friend, but she was driving him nuts. After all, she was to blame for half the complications in his life right now, all because of that stupid Tell-All questionnaire.

Josh turned and, without so much as a greeting, hurried away from her.

"Hey!" he heard Kiley yell as he took off down the hall. "Hey, Josh, get back here!"

CHAPTER 18

Crisis for Anne

Tell-All Question 38: What makes you cry?

Anne sat in the classroom, weighed down with a horrible feeling she recognized as pure and simple guilt. Guilt that she had not gathered the courage to apologize and explain to Josh about her horrible Tell-All answers—especially after reading Josh's shocking answer to Question 50. Guilt that she had taken out her embarrassment by yelling at Kiley last Friday. And the absolute worst guilt of all about something else. Something big.

Then came Dr. Wu's morning announcement. Anne could feel her face go pale.

Dr. Wu was telling all about the locker in the sixth-grade wing that had been glued shut.

"So if anyone has any information about the incident,

we expect you to come forward," the principal's voice thundered over the intercom. "For here at Harper Lee Elementary, we live by the principles of honesty and integrity, caring and responsibility..."

Anne understood, at that moment, what was the right thing to do. She just didn't know if she could do it. But how could she allow poor T.J. to be punished, to miss the best thing ever—fifth-grade camp—when she knew, she *knew* he was innocent. Her stomach ached. She felt cold and hot all at once. She felt like she had the flu all over again.

Anne raised her hand. "May I be excused for a moment?" And when the teacher nodded, Anne bolted out the door.

CHAPTER 19

Cold Shoulder for Kiley

Tell-All Question 36: What makes you mad?

Kiley steamed. First, just this morning, Josh had come out of the boys' bathroom, bumped right into her, then hurried off without so much as an "excuse me." Now, as Kiley carried the class attendance sheet to the office, Anne rushed by as if Kiley were invisible.

Kiley didn't bother to call after Anne. After all, didn't Anne owe her an apology? Because just last Friday, Anne had the nerve to yell at her about passing around the Tell-All answers. *Just what had Anne expected?* Kiley fumed. That the answers would be locked up in a vault somewhere?

And then there was the other Tell-All member, T.J.

Well, T.J. had been avoiding her for days, even in Mr. Garcia's class, ever since she had left the chalk message on his driveway—the message he probably still thought was from Katie.

I should never have started a club with those three, Kiley thought angrily as she stomped down the hall.

CHAPTER 20

Confessions for T.J.

Tell-All Question 29: What's the most surprising thing that has happened to you lately?

T.J. stood in the principal's office as Dr. Wu made her morning announcement. As she talked through the intercom about the locker incident, T.J., for a split second, thought about pretending to be guilty. That, at least, would take care of one issue: he wouldn't be allowed to go to camp.

But he heard Dr. Wu's words about honesty and integrity. And he glanced at his grandmother, who stood looking grim. Dr. Wu's announcement, had, in a way, been his grandmother's idea. His grandmother had stormed into the office this morning and insisted that finding a glue tube in one's locker did not make one the guilty party. And she had been right about that.

T.J. sighed. His grandmother so wanted him to

be a good kid. He had already racked up a couple of detentions this year. He couldn't break her heart again, he couldn't fib about this and take the blame, especially when he really *was* innocent. So T.J. just kept quiet.

Anyway, what are the chances someone will turn himself in? thought T.J. *What are the chances someone will admit to gluing Steve-O's locker shut, when all the evidence seems to point to me?*

So T.J. felt shock, total shock when the principal's doors burst open, and in rushed, of all people...Anne!

Anne took one look at Dr. Wu and T.J. and his grandmother, and burst into tears.

"Calm down, Anne," Dr. Wu commanded. "Do you have something to say?"

Anne nodded, but wouldn't stop crying.

Then the door opened a second time. And some little kid walked in.

"Alan!" T.J. heard Anne cry out with something like relief, and then Anne sank into the nearest chair.

The little guy blinked twice. "I did it," he said calmly. "And I'm not sorry," he added.

T.J. glanced again at his grandmother, who was now aiming a triumphant "I told you so" look at Dr. Wu.

Then Anne took a gasp of air and her words tumbled out in a big, crazy rush.

"Okay so Alan, my brother, well he told me he had some plot to get back at Steve-O, you know, for sitting on his project, and I told Alan not to 'cause I told him revenge was never a good thing, and then yesterday I heard about Steve-O's locker and T.J., and I didn't think that sounded like something T.J. would do but I know he gets in trouble sometimes, then at home I saw the glue cap stuck to Alan's scarf and I figured out what really happened and I was going to say something, really I was, but I didn't know how and—"

"All right Anne," said Dr. Wu. "That's enough. We want to hear from your brother now."

So T.J. watched the little guy, Alan, blink twice. Then Alan explained how he had slipped away from Anne after they walked to school together, and how he had squeezed glue through the cracks of Steve-O's locker.

"Then I threw the glue tube into the first open locker I saw," Alan finished.

Dr. Wu crossed her arms. "And that's how poor T.J. got dragged into this," she said.

"I didn't mean to get him in trouble," Alan said defensively.

"But what you did, that's vandalism to school property, you know," Dr. Wu said sternly. Alan's eyes grew wide. And Anne burst into tears again.

Dr. Wu turned to T.J. and his grandmother.

"I apologize to you both for this misunderstanding, and thank you for meeting with me this morning," she said, walking them to the door. "T.J., of course, may go back to class."

"Well," said his grandmother when they were out of

the office. "That was certainly interesting! Who would have thought that little boy would be behind all this?"

T.J. nodded, but noted something strangely cheerful in his grandmother's voice.

He knew his grandmother was relieved that he wasn't in trouble. He knew it made her sad when he got blamed for things. But there was something else behind his grandmother's happy mood.

Then it dawned on T.J..

He had been proven innocent. He wouldn't have any privileges taken away after all.

"So I guess now that I'm not in trouble..." T.J. began, and his grandmother's face broke into a bright grin.

"I guess," T.J. said slowly, feeling a tiny twinge of panic, "that means I'm going to camp."

PART 2
All Together Now:
Camp Kindred Spirits

CHAPTER  **21**

Welcome, Campers

"Hey, I want a top bunk," Josh said.

T.J. stood not far from Josh in the large wooden cabin. Both Josh and T.J. had been assigned to the Wolverine cabin at Camp Kindred Spirits with lots of other boys. Their teacher Mr. Garcia and a parent, Mr. Hagimihalis, would stay there, too. Bunk beds stood in rows inside the chilly, woodsy-smelling room.

Josh was grinning for all he was worth. So was every other kid. T.J. was not.

"Bottom bunk is fine with me," said T.J. carelessly. He noted a look of surprise—or maybe it was relief—on Josh's face when T.J. claimed the bunk under him. *He probably thinks I'm mad at him for what his brother did,* T.J. guessed. But he wasn't mad at Steve-O. He had much more important things to worry about.

T.J. glanced around the cabin. A carving of a
wolverine hung above the door. He saw a dead spider on
the wooden sill.

I'm here because I told the truth, thought T.J. *Somehow,
I always get punished even when I'm innocent.*

But he couldn't lie to his grandmother, or to Dr. Wu.
And this was the consequence. Now T.J. was here, at
camp, where he totally didn't want to be.

Camp was exactly where Josh wanted to be. Away
from Steve-O, away from his mom's do-gooding attempts
to smooth things over. And now that T.J. didn't seem to
be holding a grudge, the only problem camp offered was
how to avoid the one other person, besides Steve-O, who
couldn't stand him. How to avoid, for four days, Anne
Park. The ex-friend who had written all those rotten
things about him on her Tell-All questionnaire.

Across the road in the Cardinal cabin, Anne tossed
her sleeping bag onto the bottom bunk. She had so
looked forward to camp, but now something else,
something deep down, had doused her excitement.

In the course of a couple of months, her whole image
of herself had changed—and not for the better. She had
always thought of herself—and of her whole family for
that matter—as, well, nice. Polite, considerate, kind
to strangers. When a disaster hit somewhere in the
world, they always watched the news, worried about the
people and sent a donation. But *were* they nice, really?
And was she? First, she had done nasty things to Josh,

and then written all those cruel things on the Tell-All questionnaire. Then her mom had turned so cold to Mrs. Bendle when she had brought the peace offering of a pie. Now Alan had done something really mean to Steve-O. And worse, Alan had almost let T.J. take the blame. No, Anne corrected herself. Even worse than that. Alan practically framed T.J.

I should have paid more attention when Alan talked to me about revenge, thought Anne. *I'm his big sister. I should have made sure he didn't follow through on his plot against Steve-O.*

What did Dr. Wu think of her now? What did Josh think of her? What did T.J. think of her? And even Kiley was barely speaking to her, because Anne had yelled at her for giving Josh her terrible Tell-All answers.

"I never said we were going to keep the answers from each other," Kiley had said that day with a sniff. "In fact, that was kind of the point, Anne—to share our secrets."

And what had Josh meant about his answer, that he "really, really" liked Annie P? Was he making fun of her, getting back at her for the bratty things she'd done?

Camp was supposed to be so great. But now Anne felt like maybe everyone here hated her. And having gorgeous hair didn't matter one jellybean when everyone thought you were just plain mean.

Kiley, smoothing out her sleeping bag on the other side of the same cabin, was glad to be at camp. Here she wasn't the ugly duckling in a family of beauties. Here she looked just about as good as everyone else. And as far as she knew, there was no Katie at camp to worry about. Maybe T.J. would even finally start to really notice her.

Dr. Wu ducked her head into the cabin. "Meeting for everyone at the fire pit in five minutes."

Well, here goes, thought Kiley. She glanced across the cabin at Anne, who had chosen a bunk near the front door with its carving of a bird—a cardinal. Anne seemed to want to be as far away from her as possible. Kiley knew Josh and Anne were both still a bit mad at her for sharing the Tell-All answers, so she had avoided them for the last couple of weeks. Now they'd all be all together at the big meeting. Kiley shrugged. But that didn't matter so much. She was thinking mostly about T.J.

CHAPTER 22

Everybody Dances

Dr. Wu stood before the fire pit, clasping her hands together.

"First," she said, "Let me tell you about the exciting things we have planned for you this week. We have some fascinating programs you'll attend in the Nature Center. And we've got a local artist, John Forrest—yes, that's his real name—here to teach you all about capturing the natural world in pencil sketches. Then, of course, there's the big dance."

Kiley's eyebrows flew up. Dr. Wu paused, obviously for effect, as some of the kids mumbled or grumbled. "You're all going to learn the fine art of square dancing," she announced.

A slight groan went up from the boys.

"You've got till tomorrow night to choose a partner, or we'll pair you up, boy-girl, boy-girl. And no excuses," Dr. Wu continued. "Everybody dances!"

"Now, we're going to have a lot going on—hiking, sledding, clean-up chores—but we'll have some free time for you, too. And there," she swept her arm dramatically, "is the latest addition to camp, just put up this summer."

All eyes turned, and there, in the distance behind the cabins where he hadn't noticed them before, Josh saw them.

"Basketball courts," Dr. Wu said. "I know there's a whole group of you that likes to spend lunchtime recess shooting hoops each day."

A cheer went up from most the boys. Josh did not cheer.

"Now," said Dr. Wu. "Time for the fine print, also known as—the camp rules."

T.J. heard the principal drone on about "no leaving the cabins after lights out" and "all food must stay in the dining hall, because we don't want to encourage any critters," but T.J.'s mind was somewhere else. Just before he left for camp, Katie had started acting funny. Not eating her rat food, looking kind of slumpy. T.J. couldn't help worrying about her. Was she ill?

"…Oh, and another thing," Dr. Wu continued. "We're going to mix up activity groups all the time. So if your friends aren't with you for today's activities, they'll probably be in your group tomorrow or the next day. By camp's end, you'll have been in a group at least once with every other member of the fifth grade."

Yow, thought Anne. *That means I'll be stuck at least once with every person in the world who thinks I'm rotten.* This, she decided, would be a long, *long* four days.

CHAPTER 23

Surprising Themselves

John Forrest looked just like an artist should, Josh decided. He had white hair, like a grandpa, but it flowed down his back in a ponytail—unlike any grandpa Josh knew. He had a fair share of wrinkles, too. And on his big plaid jacket, Josh could see dabs of dried paint.

Mr. Forrest led them, a group of fifteen fifth-graders and Mr. Garcia, out to the edges of a marshy pond for their very first activity—the Art Experience, it was called. The campers each held sketch pads and sharpened pencils in their gloved hands. On the pond before them, five Canadian geese swam in a small part that was not frozen.

"You all know what a goose looks like," said Mr. Forrest. "But don't draw from some idea already stored in your brain. Look at these geese, and draw what you really see, right this moment." Mr. Forrest knelt on one knee in the snow, balancing his sketch pad on the other knee. Then he squinted, aimed his pencil, and with hardly a glance at the pad, began to work.

Some of the kids remained standing, cradling their sketch pads in one hand while trying to draw with the other. But Josh, and a few others he noticed, including T.J., imitated Mr. Forrest, dropping down to one knee. Josh thought it was pretty lucky that he and T.J. got to be in the same group, right off the bat.

Josh scanned the pond and picked one goose, and stared awhile. Then he pulled off his gloves and drew. He drew the goose, the pond, the cold stiff reeds fluttering around the pond, the prairie grass beyond.

He looked down at his paper.

"Whoa," he said.

Josh had drawn super heroes before. Monsters. Anime characters. He had never tried sketching nature. In contrast to the way his body wouldn't obey him when he tried to sink a shot, this time his fingers seemed to know exactly what to do as he sketched the goose, the pond, the bending prairie grasses. The control made him feel good—powerful.

Another fifth-grader, Amanda, a girl he barely knew, glanced at his pad. "Hey, Josh, that's really, really good," she said. Josh smiled at her, then looked again at his sketch.

And, Josh noted, it really *was* good.

Josh kept drawing, adding details, adding sky and clouds. Shadows, too.

He looked over at T.J. *How funny,* he thought. T.J. had laid his pencil down. Josh watched as T.J., looking oh-so-casual, reached down and grabbed a handful of the cold, dead grasses and stuffed them into his coat pocket.

T.J. caught Josh looking. T.J. shrugged. "Thought I might want to try sketching some nature during free time today," he said. "So I'll bring some along."

Josh, puzzled at first, slowly pulled his sketch pad up and hugged it to his chest. Suddenly he didn't want T.J. to see his picture. And Josh certainly didn't want to see T.J.'s sketch. *If he's that serious about drawing nature, he must really be good,* figured Josh. *And if he's that good, well, I don't want to find out that T.J.—T.J., the basketball superstar—is that much better at something than I am. Again.*

T.J. noticed Josh slowly moving away from him.

Great, thought T.J. *He's not buying my story about these dead weeds in my pocket. He just thinks I'm weird or something.* T.J. sighed. *Just great.*

Pretty lucky, thought Kiley. Her activity group got to stay inside for the first event, in the warm Nature Center for a special project—"Owl Pellet Dissection."

And who would have thought that picking apart something an owl threw up could be so fascinating? For as she moved things around with tweezers inside the ugly, dark, fuzzy pellet were bits and pieces of the things the owl ate—in this case, "Mouse bones!" Kiley cried excitedly. The Nature Center instructor looked down and nodded.

"Yes, you've got a jaw bone, and claws there, too," said the instructor. "This owl ate a mouse whole, and its body kept what it needed. It wrapped the rest in fur, so the owl's throat wouldn't be scraped, and sent it back up…"

"And out!" said Kiley. "The owl barfed it up."

"You got it," the instructor agreed. "Although we prefer the word 'regurgitated.'"

"What else do owls eat?" asked Kiley.

"Oh, moles, birds, rats," said the instructor.

Kiley picked some more through the brown wad of the pellet, and found a little leg bone.

Poor little mousey, she thought fleetingly. *But,* she reminded herself, *that's nature's way.* Fascinated, Kiley began poking through a second pellet. Finding this wilderness stuff so interesting had caught her off guard. *Maybe I'll become a forest ranger,* Kiley thought, *or a naturalist or something.*

As she left the Nature Center twenty minutes later, Josh and T.J.'s group was heading for their own Owl Pellet Dissection, their faces glowing from the cold.

"T.J.," Kiley said as he passed, looking for a conversation opener, "this project is so cool! You might find the bones of a bird or a mole. I found a little skull, with orange teeth, that I think was maybe from a mouse or, even better, a rat."

T.J. gave her an odd, cold stare. But that didn't stop Kiley from charging on and bringing up the subject she really wanted to discuss with him.

"Um, T.J.," she said, giving him a sidelong glance. "I have something very important to ask you."

CHAPTER 24

Midnight Plans

Way after lights out that night, Josh stood staring up at the dark, dark cabin ceiling. He did not expect this. Not at all. He had been on sleep-overs before with his cousins and some of the boys in his school. Why couldn't he fall asleep now? Why did all the night sounds, including Mr. Hagimihalis's snoring, sound so creepy tonight? Why, when he glanced at the door, did even the wolverine carving suddenly look threatening?

And why was a tear sneaking out from the corner of his eye?

Then he heard something else—other noises. It was T.J.'s bottom bunk, creaking, and then the sound of footsteps. Josh was so relieved to find someone else awake he almost shouted. But he caught himself in time. T.J. had left his bunk, and was kneeling now, reaching under the bunk.

"Teeej!" Josh whispered. "What are you doing?"

"Aww, geez Josh, you scared me!" T.J. whispered back. "You awake?"

"Yeah."

Josh thought he heard T.J. swear.

"Well, come on down. You might as well know. About my secret," T.J. said.

T.J.'s got a secret? Josh thought. *And he's gonna tell me?*

And Josh leapt down, right off the bunk.

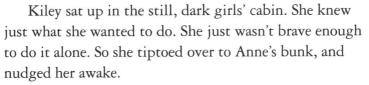

Kiley sat up in the still, dark girls' cabin. She knew just what she wanted to do. She just wasn't brave enough to do it alone. So she tiptoed over to Anne's bunk, and nudged her awake.

Anne bolted straight up.

"Don't look so scared," Kiley scolded. "It's only me."

Anne's eyes remained wide.

"Listen," said Kiley. "I need your help."

Slowly, Anne slipped from her bunk and sat on the floor next to where Kiley had dropped down.

Kiley's talking to me, Anne thought in her grogginess. *Could it be? Are things okay between us now? Maybe I have one friend who doesn't think I'm a total creep.*

"What, what is it?" Anne asked.

"Okay, here's the story," said Kiley. "Today, at the

Nature Center, I asked T.J. if he'd be my partner for the square dance."

"You did?" Anne marveled at Kiley's bravery.

"And I said, 'Why not, T.J.? After all, Katie isn't here, and you need someone to dance with.'"

"So..."

"So," said Kiley, "he said, 'How do you know Katie isn't here?' And I said, 'Well, is she?' And he said... nothing. He just kind of lifted his eyebrow, like he had some great secret."

"Yeah?" Anne put in, not sure what else to say.

"So then I got it. I figured it all out. All along I thought he liked some girl named Katie. But now I think it's some kind of cute thing between them. T.J. isn't calling her *Katie*, he's calling her *K.T.*, her two initials, just like his name, T.J. So I figure there's at least seven girls in the fifth grade with a first name that starts with K—Kara and Kendra and Kimberly and Katja and some others. All I have to do is find out which of those girls has a middle name that starts with T."

"So you're going to ask them?" Anne said. "Now?"

"Nah, too obvious. I've got a better idea."

"Okay..." Anne said hesitantly, wondering where this whole thing was going. And why it had to take place at this hour of the night.

"All we have to do is go across the path to the Caribou cabin, where Dr. Wu is staying, and grab her leather bag with all the class emergency forms. They list everything about each kid, including middle names. I remember watching my mom fill it out."

"That's crazy!" Anne said. "If they catch us leaving this cabin, they'll kick us out of camp!"

"Everyone's asleep," said Kiley, in the most soothing whisper she could muster. "We'll just take a quick look, and bring the bag right back. Come on, Anne. You're my best friend and I need your help."

And at the sound of the word "friend," Anne felt herself weaken.

I still have a friend, thought Anne. *Someone who doesn't think I'm completely horrible.*

CHAPTER  25

Prowling About

When T.J. had said he had a secret, Josh had never expected this.

No, not in a million years.

Now Josh knelt beside T.J. as T.J. pulled out a shoebox-sized plastic container from under the bed. Punched holes dotted the cover.

"T.J.," Josh whispered. "Is that who I think it is?"

"It's Katie."

"You brought your rat!"

"Shhhhh! Geez, Josh, what part of 'secret' don't you understand?"

"Sorry. Why did you bring her?"

"She seemed kind of out of it at home. Sick, maybe. I was afraid to leave her. See, when I leave home...things happen."

Josh was about to ask what kind of things when T.J. murmured, "Oh, man. Not good."

"What?"

"The lid is loose."

Carefully, T.J. lifted the lid. Josh saw a bunch of dried weeds—exactly like the ones T.J. had stuffed in his pocket for his supposed art drawings. So that's what the weeds were for! He saw a few scraps from that night's dinner, too. But what Josh didn't see was any sign of a rat.

"She's gone," T.J. said, falling back with a groan. "I can't believe she's gone!"

"Oh," said Josh.

"Do you think she's still here in the cabin?"

"Uh…"

"Grab your flashlight, Josh. Let's look."

Josh scrambled over to his duffel bag and drew out his flashlight. Together he and T.J. crawled along the cabin floor, flashing the lights under beds. Sometimes Josh's beam skimmed across a spider or June bug—and it creeped him out. But no one else woke up—that was a good thing. Still, they found nothing.

Then T.J. went to the cabin door. He opened it, and Josh could see clouds outlined in hazy moonlight.

"There's owls out here," said T.J. "And other predators. What if…what if Katie's out there?"

"Uh…"

"Josh, we have to go out there. We have to look for her."

"I'm staying here," Josh said.

"Not me," said T.J. He grabbed his coat off a peg and picked up a pair of boots from the pile by the door and pulled them on. "I'm going." And T.J. slipped out.

"But it's breaking the rules…" Josh began.

The sudden silence after the door creaked closed made Josh shiver. There was no way he could sleep now, not with T.J. out there, and possibly a rat roaming the place, and all the scary sounds inside and outside the cabin.

Then Mr. Hagimihalis let out with such a loud, startling snore that Josh grabbed his coat and boots and bolted right under the scary Wolverine carving, out the door and after T.J.

Anne couldn't believe she was outside of her cabin, at night, in a camp surrounded by tall, creepy, bony trees.

Now I know I'm a rotten person, Anne thought. *A big old rule-breaker.*

Anne didn't know what frightened her most—the idea that she might get caught, or that Big Foot might come tearing out of those woods any second.

Even Kiley seemed nervous, now that they were actually outside.

Kiley did find things spookier and the night darker than she had expected. *I won't look at Anne*, Kiley told herself. *Because I know when Anne's nervous, her face turns ghost white, and that will only make me more scared.*

"Come on," Kiley said with false bravery. "Dr. Wu's cabin is this way. We have to find this K.T."

CHAPTER 26

Into the Night

"We have to find Katie," T.J. mumbled. "We *have* to."

"Uh-huh," Josh agreed numbly.

He couldn't believe how loud his footsteps and T.J.'s footsteps sounded in the snow. Like a herd of elephants crunching around. Josh expected every parent and every teacher to come charging out of the cabins any minute. Or something else—something worse—to find them alone out there.

I've just seen too many horror movies, Josh thought, glancing behind his shoulder.

"Check the snow," T.J. instructed, running his flashlight's beam just outside the cabin door. "Look for rat prints."

But the ground near the door had been too trampled by all the campers' boots.

And so they walked, farther and farther from the Wolverine cabin.

The trees swayed. The wind whistled.

Then Josh heard something else. A crunching sound. His head flew up. T.J. heard it, too.

Two dark shapes appeared in the night, trampling through the snow and heading straight toward them.

"We've got to get out of here!" Josh cried.

But T.J. froze.

Josh grabbed T.J.'s arm and tried to pull him, but T.J. didn't budge.

He's too scared to move, thought Josh. *What am I gonna do?*

Then, slowly, T.J. lifted his flashlight and aimed it straight at the two menacing shapes.

Anne had never, ever been as petrified as she felt at that moment. The light shining in her face made her eyes tear, and in a flash, every horrible possibility about what that light could mean ran through her brain—a teacher catching her outside, a monster, an alien!

She felt Kiley's gloved hand clasp her own.

Both girls stood trembling.

Then, in an instant, the light fell from their rounded eyes and turned skyward, down, and up onto a familiar but devilishly grinning face.

CHAPTER 27

Safe?

An eye on the face winked.

"Hi, girls!" the face said.

"T.J.!" Kiley whispered back, her voice catching. And she felt both a stunning relief and a thrill rush through her. Now she was really shaking.

"And Josh," T.J. said, sending the light beam onto his accomplice's face.

"Oh my gosh, oh my gosh, oh my gosh," said Anne weakly, catching herself just before she collapsed into the snow.

"What are you guys doing out here?" asked Kiley.

"What are *you* two doing out here?" Josh shot right back.

Kiley ignored the question. "I can't believe this!" she said, changing the subject. "Look, it's all of us! It's the whole Tell-All Club."

"The Tell-All Club, is it?" a voice thundered. A decidedly stern and very adult voice. "The Tell-All Club? Is that what you call yourselves?"

The four turned slowly toward the voice.

"Well then, Tell-All Club," the voice continued. "You're going to come with me right now—and tell everything."

Once again, T.J. pointed his flashlight beam. And this time the light revealed the face of a scowling Dr. Wu.

CHAPTER 28

All Together and All in Trouble

"Ah, we're dead meat now," Josh groaned.

The four Tell-All Club members sat in a circle together on a wooden floor.

Moments before they had been herded down the road from their cabins, past the dining hall and into the back room of the ranger's station while their fate was decided. Josh, T.J., Anne and Kiley had all been called into the office individually to tell their sides of the story. Now in the front area, where the telephone sat on the ranger's counter and the clock ticked away past midnight, the principal, Dr. Wu, Mr. Garcia, and the school counselor, Mrs. Bellos-Snow, began calling their parents. And discussing their fate. They could hear the adults' low voices rumbling on the other side of the door.

"So," said Kiley glumly. "What were you two doing outside?"

"Looking for Katie," T.J. answered glumly. "I hid her in the cabin and somehow, she slipped out."

"You hid K.T. in your cabin?" Kiley said. She felt herself stiffen with shock. "You hid a girl?"

"Katie is T.J.'s pet rat, Kiley," Josh said.

Anne stopped her sniffling for a moment and began to giggle.

"She's a rat!" Anne managed between little gasps of air. "All this time you've been...and it was a rat!"

Kiley reddened.

"Listen, it's not funny right now, because she's missing," said T.J. "She's not a wild animal, you know. She won't know what to do out there." He shrugged his shoulder toward a window and the dark woods outside. All four looked out the window, then their gazes moved to the stuffed great horned owl displayed on a ledge above them.

Anne stopped giggling abruptly. Kiley turned back to T.J. and looked at him hard.

"Why did you bring her?" Kiley demanded.

And suddenly—much to everyone else's disbelief—a tear trickled out from T.J.'s eye. And he let it fall. He didn't even try to wipe it away.

For the first time, T.J. realized, he wanted to tell someone. Everyone. At least, everyone right in this room at this time.

Anne, Josh, and Kiley exchanged quick looks. Here was a side of T.J. they had never, ever seen before.

Anne reached out and touched his shoulder.

"What is it?" she asked.

T.J. took a deep breath, and told. Everything.

"See, once, when I was away from home, my dad, he just left. The second time I went away, my mom—my mom died," he said. "You know, that's why I live with my grandmother."

"Oh," said Kiley.

"Well, then Katie was acting sick..." T.J. continued. He stopped as another tear rolled down his face.

"And you didn't want to go away this time and lose her," this, from Kiley.

T.J. looked up at her. "Yeah," he said, feeling a tremendous relief at letting his secret go. "That's it. This is the first time I've gone away from home since my mom..." He left the rest unsaid.

"I remember hearing another kid say you never made it to his sleep-over birthday party," said Josh thoughtfully. "So... so that's why."

Kiley touched T.J.'s other arm. "Anyone would feel that way," she said.

"Yeah, they would," Anne agreed.

"Don't tell anyone else about...about this, okay?" T.J. murmured.

"Don't worry," said Josh.

"Yeah, let's make that the rule of the Tell-All Club. We can't tell each others' secrets to the other kids," said Kiley.

"But see now, I've just made things worse," said T.J. "'Cause the thing I was afraid of most has happened. I've lost her. I've lost Katie."

T.J. put his hands over his face and went silent.

Kiley and Anne dropped their hands from his shoulders and looked at each other.

The faint click of a phone being hung up sounded through the glass.

Josh scooted up and peeked through the window separating the two rooms. The adults were nodding yes, then no. No one was smiling.

"Oh, Steve-O's gonna love this," Josh muttered. "For once, I'm the one in deep, deep trouble."

CHAPTER 29

The Tell-All Club Tells All

"Are they coming?" asked Kiley.

"No, not yet," Josh said, sliding back down to the wooden floor with the others.

T.J. still sat with his hands covering his face.

"Anne, you are so pale," Kiley said nervously. "Don't worry. You won't get in trouble."

Anne felt an angry answer rising inside her, all about how she wouldn't be in any trouble at all if she just hadn't let Kiley talk her into...

"You're too sweet and too pretty and too nice, Anne. How could anyone stay mad at you?" Kiley asked.

Anne's ears perked up. She didn't care about pretty, but...

"You think I'm nice?" she asked.

"Everybody does," said Kiley. "That's why everyone likes you."

"Everybody *doesn't* like me," said Anne. "When I first moved here, no one even noticed me. It wasn't until I grew my hair long…"

"Hair?" said Kiley. "What does hair have to do with anything? It just took everyone a while to get to know you. Besides, not everyone ignored you. Weren't you and Josh, like, friends right away?"

"I wish we still were friends," Josh mumbled.

"You want to be friends with me?" Anne asked, feeling a warm jolt of surprise. "After all the nasty things I wrote on that Tell-All sheet?"

"Yeah, that kind of hurt. I figured out you were just mad, though," said Josh. "I just didn't know why."

Anne tried to think back. Why, exactly, had she been mad that first time?

"I think it had something to do with something Steve-O said that day you were shooting baskets in your driveway," Anne mused aloud. "And how you answered. You said 'I can't stand her,' or something like that. And it hurt."

Josh let out a short burst. "Steve-O! Every problem in my life starts with Steve-O."

"Is he really that bad?" asked Kiley.

"Yeah. But it's not just him," Josh said. He stood, and moved toward the stuffed owl. He noted the piercing golden eyes. He reached out a finger and touched the tips of its talons.

"Everyone thinks we're the perfect family, with one

problem child. But things aren't perfect. My parents—they don't want to admit Steve-O has problems. So they don't get help. And they try to fix everything themselves. At least my mom does. With pies."

"So why don't you say something?" asked Kiley.

Josh dropped back to the floor. "To my parents? I don't want to cause them more problems. Steve-O gives my parents so much trouble, I feel like I have to be perfect. At everything. Perfect manners, perfect grades, perfect attendance, even perfect at basketball."

"You could talk to Mrs. Bellos-Snow," said Anne. "She's a great counselor. My parents had Alan talk to her after...after...well, after what he did to your brother. "

"Maybe," said Josh.

The four heard movement from the other room.

Dr. Wu, still unsmiling, opened the door. She cleared her throat.

T.J. dropped his hands, and the others leaned forward.

"I have some news," Dr. Wu announced.

CHAPTER 30

A Job for the Tell-All Club

"The news is for you, T.J.," Dr. Wu began. "I've heard it over the walkie-talkie. Your rat has been found—in Mr. Hagimihalis's candy bar stash. Apparently, Mr. H. went for a midnight snack, and there she was. He put a bucket over your pet and called us."

T.J.'s face completely changed.

"She's okay?" he asked.

"Safe," said Dr. Wu. "And awaiting you, under a bucket."

"But I thought we weren't allowed to bring candy bars to…" Josh said.

"That's right. Which is why Mr. Hagimihalis is getting reprimanded, too." Dr. Wu rolled her eyes. "It's been a long night," she said. "Come in, all of you. We need to talk."

"But Katie…" T.J. began.

"Don't worry," said Dr. Wu. "This won't take long. Then you can put her safely back in her box."

The four fifth-graders stood up and shuffled into the next room, T.J. taking one last look back at the stuffed owl as they left. They took seats on folding chairs before the principal, counselor, and teacher.

"First, let me stress how serious this offense is. Initially, we had decided to send you all home," Dr. Wu began. "But T.J., we realize it was concern for your pet that led you to leave the cabin. We phoned your grandmother first, and she described to us your deep affection for your pet—and some special circumstances. So on second consideration, we decided not to banish you from camp."

Dr. Wu turned sharply toward Kiley. "Young lady, your motives for leaving the cabin and dragging Anne with you weren't quite so noble." Kiley blushed, and Dr. Wu sighed. "However, if we don't send T.J. home, we can't very well send you or Anne or Josh home, either."

The four guilty fifth-graders looked at each other with surprise.

"But you will face a punishment," Dr. Wu continued. Mr. Garcia and Mrs. Bellos-Snow nodded along.

"Tomorrow evening, you *will* NOT be attending the after dinner s'more-making party around the fire pit. Instead, the Tell-All Club will be the Scrub-All Club, responsible for scouring all the dinner pots and pans, with supervision from another rule-breaker, Mr. Hagimahalis. Fair enough?"

"More than fair," Anne squeaked.

"Thank you for not sending us home," said Josh.

"What about the square dance?" asked Kiley timidly.

"You'll be expected to finish the dishes and report to the Activity Hall for the square dance promptly at eight pm. Remember what I said—everybody dances," Dr. Wu commanded.

"And Katie?" asked T.J.

"I'm heading back to school tomorrow," said Mrs. Bellos-Snow. "I'll drop Katie at your grandmother's. Your grandmother said she'd take Katie to the vet to have her checked out." Mrs. Bellos-Snow smiled. "Don't worry. T.J. I'll take good care of her. I like rats. I had a pet rat, too, when I was a kid."

"You did?" asked T.J. "Thanks, then."

"Now, follow us," Dr. Wu said wearily. "You all are reporting back to your cabins immediately. And getting some sleep."

The Tell-All Club members rose and headed for the door behind Dr. Wu, Mr. Garcia, and Mrs. Bellos-Snow.

Josh, for a moment, caught up with Mrs. Bellos-Snow. He had liked how understanding she had seemed when she spoke to T.J. about his pet.

"When we get back, can I talk to you about—something. About my family?"

"I'm glad you asked, Josh," Mrs. Bellos-Snow said.

Josh nodded, then turned and waited for the others.

"I'm sure Dr. Wu will get a pie after all this," Josh whispered as he drew next to Anne, who giggled in reply.

Outside, the air felt brisk and the snow scrunched under their boots. Anne drew her pink scarf about her face. T.J. stuffed his hands in his pockets, forgetting that his pockets were already stuffed with the grasses, weeds, and food scraps he had collected for Katie.

"Why is Dr. Wu walking so far ahead?" Kiley asked. Her words came out with little puffs of steam.

"She's tired. She wants to get back to bed, I bet. Besides, we're good kids. They trust us back here," said Josh.

"Good kids, huh?" T.J. said, cracking a shy smile for some reason.

The four walked silently for a moment, their flashlight beams bobbing ahead of them in the still, dark night.

"You know, this whole thing has been crazy," said T.J. "All my life, I've gotten in trouble for things I *didn't* do. Now I go and break tons of rules, and I'm getting off with just washing a few dishes?"

"AND NO S'MORES!" Anne, Kiley, and Josh said together.

"Yeah," T.J. said, smiling. "I forgot. No s'mores."

"I told you, that's 'cause they know we're good kids," said Josh. "For most of us, this is the first time we've ever been in trouble at school."

T.J. stayed silent, thinking about that one.

In the moonlight, past the dining hall and just ahead, the outline of the basketball hoops showed black against the sky. As they neared, T.J. packed up a snowball, ran to the net, and sent it through. It smashed on the cement under the net.

"Not bad for a good kid," he said to himself.

Then Kiley scooped up a basketball that had been left out in the snow. She threw it to Josh.

"Nah," Josh said. "I'll pass."

And he did pass—right to Anne. Anne caught the ball, and sent it swishing through the net on the first try.

"You sure you don't want a try, Josh?" asked Kiley, who caught the ricocheting ball. "You love basketball more than anyone I know."

"Wrong," said T.J. "Way wrong. Josh doesn't love basketball. He hates it."

Josh turned quickly toward T.J. "You knew?"

"What are you talking about?" asked Kiley.

"I figured it out," said T.J. "I could tell you were just going through the motions, trying to shoot hoops 'cause that's what the other guys were doing. But," T.J. said, turning to the others, "he's killer at drawing. Amanda told me. She saw your work today."

"She told you that?" A smile spread over Josh's face.

"And then, at free time, I saw you sketching the tree outside the window."

"Yeah," said Josh. "Something happened at free time. Something big. I didn't expect it or plan, but I took my sketch pad, and on the front wrote 'EVERYDAY ART.' And then I knew. That's what I'm going to do."

"What do you mean?" asked Anne.

"I'm not shivering out there in the cold anymore doing something I can't stand like basketball," said Josh. "Instead, I'm going to draw one picture a day. And I know I'll stick to it, 'cause I stuck to my promise of shooting hoops, which I hated."

"In a year, you'll have more than three hundred drawings," said Anne. "And you'll probably get even better with each sketch."

"Good plan," said T.J. "Now, how about for old time's sake?" And T.J. stole the ball from Kiley and threw it to Josh. Josh turned, centered himself—and sunk it. Perfectly.

A cheer from the other three Tell-All members echoed through the night.

"See?" said T.J. "I told you I could teach you."

Dr. Wu turned at the sound of the cheer. She gave a stern look and a wave of her arm that clearly stated, "Come on."

"We'd better hurry," Anne said nervously. "Dr. Wu and the others are getting way ahead of us."

"Yeah," said Josh. "Let's catch up."

As they moved back to the path, Anne spoke up.

"Hey, Kiley, just one last thing I've been wondering about. You saw all our Tell-All answers. When are we going to see yours?"

"Ah…"

Anne gasped. "You never filled one out, did you?" she accused.

"Not exactly."

"WHAT!" Anne exclaimed.

Kiley took a deep breath. In the cover of darkness, it was easier to admit it all. And so she blurted out the truth.

"I kind of invented the Tell-All questionnaire for one reason. I wanted to find out if T.J. liked me."

"You put us through all of those dumb questions just to find out if T.J. liked you?" Josh cried.

"Oh, Kiley, that's low," said Anne.

"I like you," T.J. said suddenly.

"What?"

"I like you."

"You mean you like-like me?" asked Kiley carefully.

"What does that mean?" asked T.J.

"Girlfriend-boyfriend type liking," said Anne, impatient with the word games.

"Oh…" said T.J.

"No," Kiley said with a rush. "I'm sure you don't. I'm not pretty or anything. Not like my sister. Not like Ginger."

"Who says you're not pretty?" Anne said.

"I've never seen your sister," said T.J. with a shrug. "I'm just not thinking about girlfriends or stuff like that right now. But I like how you look. And I like how you're usually friendly and glad to see me—like Katie." He gave her a little nudge to the ribs. "And I think you're interesting."

"Yeah?"

"Full of all kinds of surprises inside. Like an owl pellet."

Kiley's eyebrows shot up, but she laughed. Never in a million years did she think she'd feel so warm and happy about being compared to a rat and something an owl threw up.

T.J. shrugged. "And, if you want, I'll be your partner at the square dance. Why not? I have to dance with someone. You know what Dr. Wu said."

"EVERYBODY DANCES!" the other three yelled.

Then T.J. threw his arm around Kiley's shoulder and the other arm around Anne's shoulder. Anne reached out and grabbed Josh's shoulder. "Come on, old buddy," Anne said. And the four members of the Tell-All Club, walked all together, behind Dr. Wu, Mr. Garcia, and Mrs. Bellos-Snow, down the snowy road and back to their cabins.